# Death at the Swan Tavern

Veronica Vale Investigates - book 6

Kitty Kildare

Copyright © 2024 by Kitty Kildare

All rights reserved. No part of this publication may be reproduced, distributed, or transmitted in any form or by any means, including photocopying, recording, or other electronic or mechanical methods, without the prior written permission of the publisher, except as permitted by U.S. copyright law.

For permission requests, contact: kittykildare@kittykildare.com

The story, all names, characters, and incidents portrayed in this production are fictitious. No identification with actual persons (living or deceased), places, buildings, and products is intended or should be inferred.

ISBN: 978-1-915378-88-0

DEATH AT THE SWAN TAVERN

Book Cover by Victoria Cooper

# Chapter 1

"Veronica! Look at you. Have you been into battle?" My best friend, Ruby Smythe, fussed over my appearance until I gently knocked her hand away from my hair.

"I have a plan to make myself presentable. Just give me a moment to settle Benji and his friend, and stow my bag." After I got the dogs settled on the back seat, I closed the car door behind me, glad to be in the warmth. I'd been waiting on the corner of North End Road for ten chilly minutes. "I'll focus on my appearance. You focus on driving. And hurry! We don't want to be late for the party."

"But … your hair! You look a fright." Ruby was, as always, a picture of glossy-haired perfection, positively glowing with festive spirit.

"I have my hair brush and setting spray with me. By the time we reach the party, no one will know I spent my day off with some excitable pups. Now, put your foot down." It wasn't often I ordered Ruby to make haste in her giant of a car, but I despised tardiness.

Ruby tutted, before glancing over her shoulder at our four-legged companions. "I can make allowances if the pups were half as adorable as these two. Although most people with a day off so close to Christmas would spend it preparing for the festivities, not knee deep in dog treats and fur."

"As well you know, I'm not most people." I brushed through my short hair as I pointed at the snowy road. "Off we go."

Ruby pulled onto the street. "Lady M had me packing for her today. That's not my job, but her maid is off with some terrible sickness, so I had to deal with the horses and the diamonds. I'm almost too tired to attend the Drapers party."

"You're never too tired for a party." I checked my reflection in the compact mirror Ruby had passed me.

Ruby smiled as her sleek silver car purred along, taking us away from the rundown row of terraced houses north of London, where I'd spent a busy afternoon helping an over-taxed young woman with good intentions but no skills in puppy wrangling. Prior to that, I'd been in Battersea, making plans for the dogs' shelter Christmas party, which we held every year.

"Perhaps I'm feeling my age," Ruby said. "I've been dreadfully tired lately. My father told me that burning the candle at both ends would eventually catch up with me."

"Your age! You sound like my mother."

She laughed. "Perish the thought. I'll have to make up for it with lots of dancing tonight. After all, age is just a number."

The frosted roads glittered in the car's headlamps as we made our way to the festive party. My dearest friend was a dab hand behind the wheel, having been a despatch rider, among other things, during the Great

War, but I winced as the back wheels slid across a patch of ice and snow.

With a deft twist, Ruby righted us effortlessly, her face alight with excitement. "Can you believe Christmas is nearly here? A whole week of feasting, drinking, and making merry!" She reached over and squeezed my arm through the lined sleeve of my red winter coat, the woollen trim keeping me warm.

I grinned, buoyed by her cheer. "Skating on the ice. Carols, and the most enormous Christmas goose. It'll be wonderful!"

"Do you remember last year when Charles toppled on the ice and slid into the punch bowl Mitzie insisted be the centrepiece of our outdoor luncheon?" Ruby giggled at the memory. "I don't know why she bothered with refreshments. It was so cold that day, and the punch was freezing."

I smiled at the recollection. "Poor Charles. Sopping wet in front of all of us, and he was trying so hard to impress Dalilah Dewberry. And you nearly twisting your ankle attempting that figure-of-eight after one too many glasses of sherry."

"It wasn't sherry. It was champagne. Colonel Draper's finest! And if I recall, you caught me just in time or I'd have mown down the entire party. Veronica Vale, my heroine."

It wouldn't have been the first time I'd rescued the irrepressible Ruby from some mischief or other. Although she'd returned the favour on more than one occasion.

My dear Benji barked his agreement from beneath a plaid blanket laid out on the back seats. I looked over my shoulder at his tan face and wagging tail. Snuggled next to him was my most recent furry foster. Tiberius, a pale Chow Chow. The breed had become popular thanks to Queen Victoria, after she took an interest in the Wild Dog of China when a pair were on display at London Zoo.

Forty years later, people still failed to realise how high maintenance these wonderful dogs could be. Which was how I found Tiberius abandoned and starving in a London alleyway on a freezing evening when I was walking Benji. Now Tiberius was mine. Well, until he was healthy and strong, then I'd find him the perfect happy ending through my connection with the dogs' home in Battersea.

Tiberius had formed an attachment to Benji, and would often howl continuously if we left him with anyone else, which is how he came to be attending a fun Christmas party at a fancy manor house in the English countryside at Christmas. He didn't mind where he was or how noisy it was, so long as he could be near Benji.

"Whoops! Hold on." Ruby righted the car once more. "There must be more black ice under the snow. It's treacherous stuff."

"You should ease up that overeager foot, or we won't arrive in one piece with our nerves intact."

"You told me to hurry! But don't concern yourself with my driving. I once handled a tank. Did I ever tell you?"

I rolled my eyes in a good-natured show of exasperation. "No, you neglected to mention it. Was it when you were spying for the French or the English?"

"Cheeky! I can handle anything on four wheels. But if it becomes too much for you, close your eyes and think of Christmas pudding, crackling fires, and roast turkey."

The drive was perilous but thrilling, as Ruby's solid car struggled for purchase on the icy roads after a week of typically wintery British weather. Each bend threatened unwelcome adventure, yet snug inside the car with Ruby's laughter pealing and an occasional bark from Benji, even winter's chill couldn't dampen our festive spirits.

"We're nearly there, thank heaven." My nerves prickled as we navigated another patch of ice. Perhaps venturing out in such dubious conditions hadn't been the most sensible of ideas, but I did want to catch up with old friends.

"When we arrive, I'll order us port and mince pies. The chef at the Swan Tavern is magnificent. According to Mitzie, he's a Frenchman who escaped during the war and decided not to return home." Ruby made a chef kiss with her fingers. "French cuisine is amazing."

"I know all about his fine food. I recently ate at the tavern with my landlady, Aggie. It's superb cuisine." I rested a hand on my stomach. "I ought to have purchased another crepe de chine frock. They're so forgiving on one's figure."

Ruby nodded. "I'm unsure Mitzie approves of them, but I think they're smashing." She'd been wearing the flattering style for the last month, and had recently purchased several more dresses in different colours, despite her purse begging her not to. Ruby could never resist a pretty dress in a flamboyant shade.

"I'll convince Mitzie they're all the rage. She cut her hair in a shingle bob after seeing mine, so I know she's coming around to modern ways." The style was so neat and pretty and required hardly any effort compared to the torture of finger waves I'd endured when younger.

"We want to look our best. There's no telling which eligible gentlemen Mitzie has invited to entertain us. She's intent on finding us husbands." Ruby chuckled. "Although I have a feeling your heart has finally been captured. It's such a shame Jacob can't join us for the festivities."

"I'm quite content to be without him this holiday." Jacob Templeton, my close male companion, had dashed away on an important task. A task connected to his shocking discovery that my late father, Davey Vale, may have been murdered.

"Naturally, old girl, but we can't remain unmarried for too long, or those spinster rumours will spread like wildfire and we'll be tarred and feathered forever."

I studied Ruby's profile. "You've not been too badly burned since the whole business in Margate?"

She pressed her lips together, but made no reply.

I was skating over the thinnest of ice, and we'd barely talked about her whirlwind romance with the deceitful Alfonso during our recent summer holiday, but things needed to be said.

I drew in a breath, but Ruby beat me to it. "I regret what happened. All of it. And I'm sorry I was so beastly to you. I lost my head. It was silly to fall out over a man."

My heart warmed at her honesty. "I'm sorry, too. I spoke out of turn on more than one occasion. I wanted to protect you, but I said things I shouldn't."

"You were right, though! Everything you said to me. I got caught up in the moment and am left with nothing but an aching heart and lingering problems."

"Problems? Has Alfonso been in touch?" If that cad attempted a reconciliation with Ruby, I'd set Benji and Tiberius on him, and ensure they didn't let go until he was thoroughly sorry.

"Oh, no. Nothing like that. Even if he sent me the contents of a flower shop as an apology for his behaviour, I have no interest in him. Fool me once, shame on him. Fool me twice, well, you know how the saying goes." Ruby glanced at me. "But let's not talk about problems. We're celebrating Christmas, and I plan to overindulge with my closest friends and laugh until my cheeks ache."

Two pinpricks of light swung out from behind a parked van, the headlamps of the oncoming vehicle hurtling towards us at an unsuitable speed, given the conditions.

Ruby sucked in a breath and frowned. "He needs to slow down. Maybe he's late for his Christmas party."

"Or perhaps he's overestimating how well he can drive."

Ruby snorted a laugh. "I'll best anyone behind the wheel."

"It's not you I'm worried about. Look out!" I clutched my beaded purse.

Ruby gasped. The car seemed bent on a collision with us, its backend sliding out, getting ever closer. With an ear-splitting screech of brakes, Ruby skidded off the road into a powdery snowbank. My heart stuttered at our narrow escape.

The other vehicle careened past, horn blaring. "Watch where you're going!" a harsh male voice bellowed from an open window.

Pale beneath her rouge, Ruby stared at me in shock. "The very devil of the man! He thought I was to blame for his reckless driving."

Benji's bark stirred me into action, and I checked on him and Tiberius. Other than a rumpled blanket, they were fine, even more so after I'd fed them treats from my coat pocket.

"Are you quite alright?" I asked Ruby, after petting Benji and Tiberius to soothe them and me. Petting an adorable dog always made me feel better.

"I shall drive slowly the rest of the way, I think. The rudeness of some people!" Ruby eased the car back onto the road and patted the dash fondly. "You never let us down."

"You drive it like a tank, and fortunately for us, it's built like one." Her car had been an outrageously expensive gift from a former admirer, who'd hoped to trap Ruby with promises of wealth and a crumbling country manor. Fortunately for me, Ruby wasn't for trapping, nor was she a country girl, preferring the conveniences of town life to a chilly country pile far from the vibrant London parties and clubs.

"You can always rely on my driving skills." The colour returned to Ruby's cheeks as our journey continued. "We'll pass through Little Kennington soon, and then it's on to the Swan Tavern and all the food and drink we can consume. And dancing!"

"Knowing Mitzie, it'll be a nonstop party. I doubt we'll be finished before dawn," I said.

"I'm so looking forward to it." Ruby sighed. "Although it's a shame, we couldn't have the party at your house like last year. Your front parlour has that glorious fire. It's so cosy."

"With my mother's persistent cough and Matthew having another one of his turns, I thought it best to give them a peaceful time and accept Mitzie's invitation. And we have eight cats and three dogs staying at the moment, so the noise would have unsettled them."

Ruby gently swatted my arm. "Veronica! You said no more cat lodgers after that tabby left half a rodent in your favourite pair of shoes."

"And I meant it! But when I visited the Rudyard household to write Mr Ruddard's obituary, I found his widow in pieces and the cats starving. She said she'd have to drown them because she had no money to buy food." My job as an obituary writer at my uncle's newspaper took me into the often-fascinating, and sometimes tragic world of the recently departed.

"Doesn't the poor woman have children who can support her?" Ruby asked.

"Three boys, but they were all lost to the war."

"That's terribly sad. But why have so many cats if you can't afford to keep them?"

"It was Mr Ruddard who adored them. He even wrote poetry about them. His widow gave me a few of his scribblings and said I could use them in his obituary."

"Are they any good?"

"They're adorable." They were dreadful, but each line of poetry brimmed over with his admiration for fine felines, so I was happy to take them and cherish them.

Ruby glanced at me. "You abandoned the widow to her lonely fate, but you took in the unwanted cats?"

"Mrs Ruddard has a fine home. If she cuts back on her household employees, she can stay there and not go hungry. If I hadn't intervened, the cats wouldn't have been so fortunate." And I never abandoned an animal in its hour of need, which was how I came to have so many furry residents at the family home over the holidays.

"How does your mother feel about so many cats taking up residence?" Ruby asked.

"She claims they make her sick, but the last time I checked, three cats were curled up on her bed, and she was knitting them Christmas bonnets. Mother loves their company when I'm busy with work."

"We'll have to sneak her some cake from the party. Edith has a sweet tooth, just like me. Will you want to visit on Christmas Day? I don't mind driving us over, and Mitzie won't miss us for a few hours."

"Only if the weather doesn't get any worse. Blizzards were mentioned on the wireless, so I warned my mother and Matthew not to expect us, to ensure they weren't disappointed."

Ruby carefully steered around a parked omnibus, going slowly in case any passengers stumbled onto the road. "It's only a few miles from the tavern. We could always walk."

"It's a lot more than that!" I arched an eyebrow. "Besides, you despise walking."

"I despise walking in the rain! And you always drag me out when it's freezing, or too hot!"

A little weather of one extreme or the other never bothered Benji or me. A sensible coat, sturdy boots, and a pocketful of snacks for human and dog, provided for an enjoyable experience.

Ruby grinned at me. "Maybe they'll surprise you and visit the Swan Tavern. They know we're using the Swan for the gathering, don't they?"

"They do. But their arrival at that particular door would be a Christmas miracle. My mother has barely left the house since our trip to Margate. She said the fresh sea air overwhelmed her lungs. And she's been trying to convince our put upon doctor that the salt air gave her hives."

"We could arrange for someone to collect them. I could do it, so long as I go steady and don't have too much to drink. Although Mitzie is a shocker for getting everyone merry."

"My mother doesn't enjoy visiting the taverns, not anymore. There are too many memories within their walls." Memories I may need to rake up if Jacob's belief about my father's death was true.

Although I was doing my best to focus on the present and enjoy Christmas, I kept thinking about what he'd told me. Could my father's death have been caused by someone else? How should I reveal such shocking news to my family without causing them to freefall into panic and anxiety? It was the reason I'd kept the news to myself.

Ruby lifted one shoulder. "Don't underestimate the allure of a good party. Although, I hope Eddie won't be too much of a grump. He was frightfully surly the last time we met."

I chuckled to myself. Colonel Edward Draper, Eddie to his friends, came across as a no-nonsense, practical chap, with no fondness for entertaining. But I'd always respected his steadfastness and calm. It was the temperament you needed when embracing danger, something he'd done when serving in the Great War.

"Mitzie will more than compensate for his grumpiness." I released a gentle sigh of pleasure as an idyllic sight greeted us when we reached the outskirts of the charming village of Little Kennington.

Ruby slowed the car to a crawl so we might admire the scene. Street lamps glowed along snow-dusted streets, and smoke from chimneys curled skyward. Small shop windows were decked for the season with pine garlands, scarlet velvet bows, and fanciful festive displays. The bakery framed a sumptuous stacked cake topped with white frosting and sugared violets.

"Mitzie enlivens any party," Ruby said. "She even got the local Women's Institute up and dancing in their sensible flats after that deadly dull lecture on dried flowers."

"She achieved that because she spiked their tea with something, I've no doubt."

Mitzie Draper was Eddie's younger, spirited wife. I'd first encountered Eddie during my service in the Great War, and Mitzie soon after. She'd embraced me like an old friend and insisted we dine together. Mitzie was the heart of most social occasions in Little Kennington, where they had their home, and she utterly adored Eddie.

We proceeded through the village and past the frosted village green. Should I ever settle into a quiet life, this was the sort of place I'd choose, with its quaint cottages, pretty trees and green, and close-knit community. For the present, however, my family's rambling, chaotic, often fur-covered house suited me. I had my own room and indoor bathroom, and my mother took a trifle for the rent, and only when I pressed it upon her.

I'd considered renting my own home, but I was more comfortable staying with my family, so I could keep an eye on them. And there was plenty of space to pursue my passions without too much motherly interference.

"Oh, my goodness! Do you see what I see?" Ruby's eyes were wide.

A burst of laughter escaped my lips. "Swans! Seven of them. Just like the Christmas carol."

"It's a sign our stay at the Swan Tavern will be just the ticket." Ruby stopped the car as the proud white birds ambled across the road without a care in the world, knowing all would stop to grant them safe passage.

Once the remarkable sight had passed, we continued on, leaving behind Little Kennington's quaintness, and Ruby continued for several miles until the bustle of London surrounded us. Shops sparkled with Christmas delights, people hurried along the pavement with armfuls of gifts, bundled against the cold, and when I opened the window a crack, the scent of roasting chestnuts made me smile.

Ruby turned onto a private lane, thankfully cleared of snow, and a few seconds later, the Swan Tavern rose before us. Golden light spilled from the small, frosted windows, illuminating the tavern's sign of two swans, their necks entwined, swinging gently in the crisp winter breeze.

"We've arrived!" I said on a relieved exhale.

"You didn't doubt my driving for a second, did you?" Ruby gently jabbed me in the ribs.

"Not for a moment."

"Before we go inside, let me make sure you're presentable for polite company." Despite my protests, Ruby insisted on applying lipstick and blush, and rearranged my hair, even though I'd made myself look perfectly respectable. "Are you sure you can't tempt Jacob back from his adventures? You still haven't told me what's got him dashing about so much."

I was saved from responding to that awkward question as the private guest entrance to the tavern flew open, and our hostess's silhouette was etched against the welcoming glow, one hand waving vigorously. "Girls! You're here at last! Hurry inside before you freeze into beautiful ice sculptures and I make a party attraction of you. Welcome to the Swan Tavern!" Mitzie Draper fairly vibrated with excitement. "And leave your bags. Baxter will bring them inside."

"You brought your butler with you?" I asked. "Doesn't the poor fellow deserve time off at Christmas?"

"Nonsense! We go everywhere with him. I'd perish without my faithful retinue taking care of us. And it's just him. I gave the others time off, so I'm not a complete monster."

I let Benji and Tiberius out to sniff and stretch their legs, while we greeted Mitzie, and for a few seconds, I forgot about what Jacob was getting up to. And so I should. The festivities had begun! It was time to enjoy the warm embrace of Christmas with friends. Everything else would come out in the wash.

At least, I hoped it would, and no Christmas miracles would be needed to solve the mystery of what really happened to my father.

# Chapter 2

The private foyer of the Swan Tavern rang with laughter and good cheer as Ruby handed her coat to Baxter while I unfastened the dogs' leads, allowing them to explore. They never wandered far from me, my ever-faithful companions. Tiberius was less confident, and stuck close to Benji, so he could show him how things worked and who to trust.

"Isn't this thrilling?" Ruby said, her curls bobbing as she explored who had already arrived. "A party, presents, spiced punch, and handsome gentlemen. What more could a girl desire during the holidays?"

I smiled at my excitable friend. "Mitzie, you always know how to throw the perfect bash."

"It's a treat to arrange a party, darling. Well, order others around to ensure everything is splendid. And it's all thanks to you we get to have our Christmas fun here!" Mitzie wore a stunning sleeveless beaded cream tulle dress over a silk slip, the deep V-neck decorated with crystal bugle beads that shimmered with her every movement.

A faint blush warmed my cheeks. "There's no need to thank me. You needed a space, and I knew the

Swan Tavern had available rooms for guests to enjoy themselves."

"I absolutely do, since your family owns this tavern! When the heating gave up the ghost at the manor house, I worried we'd spend Christmas huddled around an open fire with only raw vegetables to eat. How miserable would that have been? Then you proposed this venue, and my heart sang with joy."

"It was my pleasure. And it gives me an opportunity to visit Aggie, my landlady, and ensure everything is shipshape for the holidays."

"You are both staying for the whole of Christmas, aren't you? I've had the rooms prepared. And I've got you gifts," Mitzie said. "I know you were undecided the last time we spoke."

"Of course we're staying," Ruby said. "Ignore Veronica's talk about work. If we weren't here, she'd insist we spend Christmas Day marching about London, looking for stray animals to feed."

"The health benefits of a vigorous walk can never be underestimated. Neither can the company of a good dog." I enjoyed being outdoors with Benji on a crisp morning. I invariably winkled out my best thoughts when walking.

"We'll take a gentle stroll after Christmas luncheon, but I'm planning a restful holiday for us all," Mitzie said. "Once tonight's rabble of guests have gone home, only a select few will remain. And I have so many things I want us to do."

I glanced about as Mitzie outlined her plans for feasting, ice skating, gift-giving, and games. It sounded like exhausting fun, but Mitzie was never happier than when arranging entertainment and making people smile. She was a consummate hostess, renowned for her parties, even during the Great War.

I'd visited the Swan Tavern many times, but it had never looked as lovely as this. Mitzie had outdone herself. The private oak-panelled entrance hall was a hive of activity. A towering Christmas tree glinted with garlands of tinsel and beads. Waiters in white tie circulated with trays of sparkling champagne and delicious nibbles, and a small band played lively tunes from the main entertaining room at the back of the tavern.

"Ladies, you must meet John. He's simply divine." Mitzie gestured to a dark-haired man lounging by the Christmas tree, drink in hand, talking to an older man with blond hair and a wisp of a moustache. "John, do meet my dearest friends, Veronica Vale and Ruby Smythe."

John nodded at the blond man, then sauntered over, tilting his whisky glass at us. "Enchante, ladies." His gaze raked over Ruby in a way that turned my stomach.

Ruby batted her eyelashes coyly. "The pleasure is ours, Mr...?"

"Robinson. But please, call me John." He moved closer to Ruby, paying me no mind.

I sighed, knowing this would end in heartbreak should Ruby take a fancy to his handsome face. And she'd had more than enough of that recently.

"Vale, stop scowling and fetch yourself a drink." Eddie Draper's gravelly voice boomed behind me. I turned to see my old friend, his walrus moustache flecked with crumbs from the mince pies.

"It's good to see you, Colonel." I walked over and gave him a quick embrace. He smelled of pipe tobacco, peppermint, and a hint of whisky.

Eddie grunted. "You, too. Although I wish I could say the same about the rest of this throng. Another boring crush, if you ask me. I'd rather be smoking cigars at my club than making small talk about the upcoming festivities."

"But you shan't sneak away to your club because you love Mitzie, and parties make her happy. I know you secretly enjoy them as well."

"Only when there are the right sort of people about." His gaze skimmed John and displeasure flickered in his eyes.

"Oh, Eddie, stop being a grump!" Mitzie joined us and batted him with a delicate hand. "Now, be a dear and mingle while I see to the games." She bustled off to arrange the party diversions.

"It was good of you to offer us the place at such short notice," he said to me, not seeming at all inclined to mingle with anyone else. "Mitzie was in tears when things went awry at the manor. But then you telephoned with a solution, and here we are. It's a damn fine place your father purchased. Money well spent, although it must have cost a pretty penny to bring it up to this standard."

"My father never scrimped on his investments." I drew in a breath. Eddie had enjoyed the occasional drink with my father when he'd visited Little Kennington. Although they hadn't been firm friends, would he know anything unusual about how he died? Everyone close to the family was aware that my father's car and his belongings had been discovered at Beachy Head, but was that the whole truth?

Eddie didn't miss my hesitation. "Is something on your mind, Vale?"

"There is. I'm gathering information about a delicate matter."

"I'm not known for my delicate conduct." He sipped from his glass. "Do you need help?"

I made a decision and shook my head. "You're more of a strategist than a clue finder."

He gently snorted. "True enough. I bark the orders and make things happen."

"Those talents were put to excellent use during the war."

"I won't deny that. Just as your talents were homed on the right area when we needed them the most."

We shared a look. Eddie knew more about what I did during the Great War than most people did . He was also discreet with that knowledge, for which I was eternally grateful.

"If there's a challenge to discuss, I'm available." Eddie scowled at a group who raucously laughed as they hurried past us. "That's if I survive this dratted party. And there's not enough whisky in this place to convince me to join in the games."

"Mitzie will insist you take part, and you can never refuse her."

He snorted. "Then I'd better move on to the brandy."

I smiled and excused myself to fetch a drink of my own, then checked the dogs were on their best behaviour, and went to see what Ruby was getting up to. I found her still conversing with John by the Christmas tree. Her cheeks were flushed, no doubt from the glass of champagne she held and the smooth compliments flowing from John's mouth.

I stepped back as a group of chattering, glittering guests dashed by. I enjoyed a party, but I preferred a few close friends to a crush of strangers. I was looking forward to tomorrow, when the party would be smaller and I hoped to have a decent conversation or two.

Ruby caught my eye and gestured me over. "We're taking part in the games!"

I arched a brow. They were a 'we' now?

She grinned and leaned close. "Lighten up! A girl needs some festive fun, especially after you know who was so awful to me in Margate. You can't say no to joining in. You're my wing woman for the night."

Before I could protest, she dragged me to the main entertainment room with John taking the rear. Mitzie was assembling couples to join in the fun and games. Ruby eagerly partnered with John while I hovered nearby, watching the interaction unfold whilst pretending to study the paintings hung on the wall. Ruby could get distracted by an attractive face and broad shoulders, and promise more than she should when the romance of the moment overtook her, so I remained close enough to ensure I overheard their conversation.

John grinned at Ruby as they waited to join in a lively game of charades. "What's your favourite film?"

Ruby tapped her chin. "The Dying Detective. I adore Sherlock Holmes."

John feigned offense. "A mystery? I prefer war films!"

"After all we've endured? Did you serve?"

"I did. I have many stories I can share with you."

"So do I! Where did you serve?"

John moved closer, lowering his voice. "Let's forget the war. I'd love to discuss Holmes over drinks, just the two of us, so we can get to know each other better. Perhaps we could go somewhere quieter later on."

Ruby blushed. "I believe drinks at a lively party best suit me. Besides, I hardly know you!"

John raised his glass in concession. "Then to a wonderful evening among friends, old and new."

I bristled at his pushy manner and attempt to separate Ruby from the group. This scoundrel required close observation. Ruby acted as if her recent heartbreak didn't bother her, but I'd been there to pick up the pieces, and it hadn't been pretty.

The games gathered pace, and Ruby displayed her acting talent, easily guessing the titles of books and films John overzealously pantomimed. At each guess, John seized upon an excuse to grab Ruby's hand or brush against her arm. She laughed it off, caught in the moment, but John was too confident in himself. It verged on unhealthy arrogance. When a man thought too much of himself, it led to trouble.

Mitzie dashed over, smiling at me, while another couple took their turn in the game. "Are you having fun?"

"Immensely." I lowered my voice and leaned in close. "How do you know John?"

"He moved to Little Kennington a few months past. Eddie met him at the pub. They had a drink together and got to swapping war stories. He has no local friends or family alive, so I invited him to stay over the holidays. You don't object, do you?"

"I'm undecided. What do you make of him?"

Mitzie arched a thin brow. "John's a hoot. But from your stern expression, I gather you don't care for him?"

"He's overly confident."

"Oh! Don't tell me you're jealous because he's not interested in you? I thought you had that policeman chasing after you. Jeffrey something or other."

I pinned her with an icy stare. "Jacob Templeton. And he's not chasing me."

She patted my arm like she was settling an anxious spaniel. "Don't be such a prickle. You could have brought Jacob with you, you know."

"He's working."

"So close to Christmas?"

"It's a private matter." I pressed my lips together. I'd scheduled a telephone call with Jacob tomorrow to discuss his progress. And although I longed to talk to someone about what he was investigating, until there was more information, there was no point in getting ahead of myself and making a fuss over what was most likely rumours and misunderstandings.

Mitzie watched the game for a few seconds before turning back to me. "We've so few eligible young men left, and I thought John amusing. But if he oversteps, tell me, and I'll ensure Eddie has a word."

I gave a curt nod.

"And try to relax, Veronica. This is a party." She squeezed my elbow and hurried off to chat with a priest who'd just arrived, looking somewhat startled by the noise and bright lights.

When Ruby went to get a glass of punch, I dashed over to John. My instincts about him wouldn't fade, and there was something I didn't like about the man. "Mr Robinson, you appear to be having a little too much fun with my friend."

John raised his palms in mock surrender. "Ruby is charming company, and she's been telling me all about you. You sound like the daring duo. She has almost as many war stories as me. I'm never certain women should have served. It's unbecoming."

Ruby returned, handing me a glass of punch and giving me a second to bite my tongue. "Whatever are you two conspiring over? If you're hoping to best me in the next round, then good luck. My competitive spirit nearly rivals Veronica's."

"I was telling our new friend how fond you are of games that don't require physical contact. Cards, perhaps?" I gave John a pointed look.

John glanced from Ruby to me, realising his false charm wasn't having the desired effect. "My apologies, Ruby. I meant no disrespect. From now on, I shall be on my best behaviour. If you'll excuse me, I must speak to Colonel Draper." He bowed his head and moved away swiftly.

Ruby watched him depart, her smile fading. "Don't fret about me. I had his measure. One more 'accidental' caress and I'd have bopped him on the nose. Thank you for watching out for me, though." She slipped her arm through my crooked elbow. "Now, no more mixing with dubious men, no matter how handsome they may be. Let's enjoy this delicious punch and stick together. How does that sound?"

I squeezed her arm, relieved she'd come to her senses where John Robinson was concerned. Ruby didn't need any more complications in her life.

We spent the next hour revelling in the charades, champagne, and charming hospitality. Mitzie was right. I could take life too seriously, but tonight, I intended to let down my hair and enjoy myself. After all, it was almost Christmas.

# Chapter 3

"If you need to escape for a few moments, I won't hold it against you." Ruby stood at the edge of the impromptu dance floor, jigging from side to side along with the jolly music.

"What makes you think I want to escape?" I asked.

Ruby smiled at me, a knowing glint in her eyes. "Because you've been looking at the door every few seconds. Don't think you have to stay because of me. In your absence, I won't misbehave. Well, not too much."

I laughed. "I trust you not to act up."

"Then go and catch your breath. I know all the noise bothers you."

"I'm enjoying the party," I said. "But I wouldn't mind a break from the hustle and bustle. It seems Mitzi has invited most of Little Kennington and a third of London to this party."

"It is overly warm. And I've had my foot trodden on twice." Ruby fanned her face.

"I'll pop to the private bar," I said, "and take Benji and Tiberius with me. Benji is fine in all manner of company, but I don't want this to overwhelm Tiberius. He's a sweet dog, but I've yet to test him in a situation as crowded as this. Although I'll need to find them first."

"The last time I saw Tiberius, he was being hand-fed sausages by a lady with a huge fur wrap and diamonds at her throat," Ruby said. "She seemed enchanted by him."

"Perhaps he's found his new home," I said. "That would be a Christmas treat. Although he'll need an experienced owner. Chow Chows are prone to skin infections."

"Don't tell her that!"

"If she's the right owner for Tiberius, she won't mind giving him special care." I looked at the door again. "I also need to see how Aggie is faring. With most of the pub closed for this private gathering, everyone will be crammed into the public bar, so she'll be run off her feet."

"Don't get involved with pulling pints and forget you're supposed to be enjoying a Christmas party," Ruby said. "Go for half an hour. But if you don't return, I'm coming to find you."

"I'll be back soon." It took me a few minutes to locate the dogs, and sure enough, a sprightly-looking elderly lady with white hair and an expensive-looking fur wrap was feeding Tiberius and Benji from her china plate. She looked up as I approached.

"Good evening. I see you're keeping excellent company at this party," I said.

The woman had bright blue eyes and a warm smile. "Are these beauties yours?"

"Benji is mine," I said. "I'm fostering Tiberius until we can find him the perfect home. Chow Chows are a special breed of dog and need careful looking after."

"I know all about that. My aunt had six! She was enamoured by them after Queen Victoria, god rest her soul, took a liking to them. She ended up employing a full-time chap to care for them. They were adorable dogs. You say this one is up for adoption?"

I nodded and formally introduced myself.

"Lady Samantha Nickerson."

"Nickerson Gold?"

"One and the same. Well, it was my father's business. My brother oversees things these days."

I drew in a breath. The Nickerson family had made a fortune in metals before specialising in gold and diamonds. It would explain the glittering gems around Lady Samantha's neck. "I volunteer at the dogs' home in Battersea. Have you heard of it?"

"I can't say I have, but we live in Mayfair. And we have a summer home in Surrey. One in Italy, too. And Kent. So many homes to keep on top of."

"Does your summer home come with land?"

"Twelve acres, give or take."

"Which would be plenty of grounds for a dog to romp around in, should you so desire."

Lady Samantha couldn't take her eyes off Tiberius. "Indeed it would."

"I'd be happy to show you around the dogs' home," I said. "I can tell you're a dog lover."

Her lined mouth puckered a fraction before she nodded. "I am looking for something to occupy my time. My husband is often away. Is this fine fellow ready for adoption?"

"Almost. Tiberius is sensitive, so he needs time to settle. Benji is an excellent companion for a nervous dog. He's showing him the ropes, and Tiberius is making tremendous strides. With the right owner, he could be ready early in the new year."

"I see Benji knows how the world works. And he's a charmer, to boot. He was the one who slunk his way over here with Tiberius behind him when he saw my plate of food. Not that he begged. He sat a respectable distance away and gave me the most adorable look. He even raised his paw. Such an angel."

"He's a mischievous angel," I said with a smile. "But I can never resist his charm."

"Write down the details of this dogs' home, my dear. Perhaps we can arrange something after Christmas," Lady Samantha said.

I was quick to do as she asked. The dogs' home was run on a shoestring and good will, so any opportunity to gather wealthy patrons was strongly pursued.

After Lady Samantha had shaken Benji's paw, laughing as she did so, and gently patted Tiberius on the head, I escorted the dogs out of the noisy party and into the bar used by the Swan Tavern's regular clientele.

As I'd predicted, the bar was busy. The drinkers were mainly male, most likely escaping the Christmas chaos at home or enjoying a quiet pint of ale after work.

It took several minutes and some gentle 'excuse me' nudging before I made it to the bar with the dogs. Aggie Smith was bustling around behind the bar, assisted by one member of staff. She was a delightfully jolly landlady—round-cheeked, rosy-faced, and with a head full of bristling curls. She'd worked at the Swan Tavern while my father was alive, and he'd only ever said pleasant things about her.

I was about to raise my hand to get her attention when I noticed John stood at the bar. What was he doing here? He should be at the party. He didn't strike me as the kind who was a shrinking violet and needed a break from the noise and music.

After calling the dogs close to my side, so nobody would trip over them, I continued watching John. He had a face like thunder and was nursing a small glass of whisky. After a moment, he gestured Aggie over. I could tell by the tight set of her shoulders that she wasn't happy to speak to him.

I was too far away to hear their conversation, but it involved Aggie shaking her head several times, her expression growing sterner by the second. Eventually, she pointed at the door, but John shook his head. She wanted him gone, but John was determined to stay. It made no sense to me why he'd be here. Surely, if he wanted to drink, there was plenty at the party and it wouldn't cost him anything. Mitzie was nothing if not a generous host.

A man shoved his way to John's side and glared at him. The conversation grew intense as the dark-haired older man jabbed a finger against John's chest, causing several people around them to back away.

I couldn't resist any longer. I pushed my way through the crowd until I was within listening distance. Benji and Tiberius stayed close to my side, sensing the tension.

"You have a nerve, coming back here," the dark-haired man said. "I told you what would happen if I saw your lying face in here again."

"It's a free country. I can drink where I like," John replied. "And I'm here with friends. I was invited."

"No one wants you here. You're trouble."

"I've done nothing to you. I just want a quiet drink on my own."

"What you need to do is leave. If you don't, you may not see Christmas Day."

John smirked into his glass. "You don't have it in you to do anything other than make empty threats."

The man shoved him. "You took what didn't belong to you."

"You knew the risks."

"Like hell I did. You promised me it was a sure thing. You said I'd double my money. Where is that money? I want it back."

"I've got nothing for you. And I promised you nothing. If you think that, you must have misheard me."

The dark-haired man shoved John again, this time so hard, he almost fell off his stool.

"That's enough, gentlemen!" Aggie, who'd been watching the confrontation, hurried around the bar. "We want no trouble here. This is a quiet pub, and people want a friendly drink and to enjoy the open fire. They don't come here to listen to drunken rabble rousers making fools of themselves."

"Aggie! He shouldn't be allowed in here. You know what he's like," the dark-haired man said.

"And I know what you're like, Nathan. I also know how many ales you've downed this evening. Go outside and walk it off. The frigid air will do you good. And while you're walking, keep going all the way home. Your wife will be wondering where you are."

"Not without my money!"

Aggie sighed. "John, can you help him? A hint of generosity at Christmas wouldn't go amiss."

"Nathan made a mistake. He should learn from it," John said.

Nathan's fist clenched, but a stern look and a sharp word from Aggie stopped him in his tracks. He heaved out a sigh and rubbed his forehead. "I don't know what I'll tell my old lady. How are we supposed to pay for Christmas?"

"You'd be able to pay for it if you didn't believe nonsense about sure things when it comes to gambling," Aggie said. "Take this. Down it, and leave." She handed Nathan a small whisky.

He grudgingly took it, swallowed it in one gulp, and wiped the back of his hand across his mouth. "I'm not done with you, John."

John raised his glass. "Merry Christmas to you, too."

Nathan glowered at him for another second, then turned and jostled his way out of the crowded pub.

After a second of silence, the customers returned to their drinks and conversation.

Aggie suddenly saw me. An enormous smile lit her face, and she dashed over, leaning close to engulf me in a warm, floral-scented hug. "Veronica Vale! I thought you'd forgotten about me, what with you getting yourself tied up in that fancy private party. A friend of the Drapers, no less. I didn't know you had such posh friends."

"We've been friends since the war. But I would never forget you." I returned her embrace with equal vigour. "You're having an interesting evening."

Aggie glanced in the direction Nathan had stormed off. "It's just high spirits and holidays. Nathan has a hot head and little sense. And how's Benji? Ooooh. Who's his handsome friend?" She adored dogs almost as much as I did and spent a minute petting both of them.

"I was wondering if you would keep an eye on Benji and Tiberius for me," I said. "The private party is getting raucous, and I have a feeling it'll go on until the small hours. These dogs need their rest."

"They're always welcome here. And I'll be going to your dogs' home after Christmas to adopt myself two new ones. This place feels so empty since I lost Jip and Rocky."

"There'll be plenty of adorable faces for you to choose from," I said. "Sadly, people often get rid of the older dogs to make room for younger ones at Christmas."

"I'm happy to have an older one. They'd fit in with my lifestyle perfectly. We can complain about our aching joints together." She gave a hearty laugh.

"We'll find you the ideal dog." I glanced at John and feigned surprise. "Mr Robinson! You're not enjoying the party next door?"

He glanced at me, a sullen look on his face. "I needed a break. There's nothing wrong with that, is there?"

"Absolutely not." Perhaps he was nursing a bruised ego after Ruby's rejection.

He finished his drink, pushed away from the bar with a nod, and left, most likely returning to the party.

"Your conversation with John didn't look friendly. Is he causing you trouble?" I asked Aggie.

"Oh, it was something and nothing."

"You didn't look happy with him."

"He keeps pressing to have a tab. But I told him, no credit. No one gets credit in this pub."

"Do you know John well?"

"Well enough to know he doesn't always pay his bills, and when he does, he comes up short and is several weeks late. I run a tight business here and I won't have anyone taking advantage of me. Or you."

"Quite right, too," I said.

"That doesn't mean he won't try his luck every time he comes in here," Aggie said. "I wish he'd stay in Little Kennington and bother the landlord there. But he often comes into town for business."

"What kind of business is he in?"

"The morally grey kind," Aggie said. "I don't ask too many questions."

"Was that why he was arguing with that other gentleman?"

"Most likely." Aggie's eyes widened. "You don't have a fancy for John, do you?"

"Good grief. No!"

"But you have an interest in him?"

"A healthy caution," I said. "His conversation with Nathan was heated."

"It will get heated when you're foolish enough to use your Christmas pot to bet on an old nag John promised would be a sure thing. As if there's any such thing." Aggie shook her head. "Anyway, can I get you a drink while you're here?"

"No, but thank you," I said.

"I suppose with your busy social calendar, I'll see no more of you over Christmas." Aggie returned to the other side of the bar to deal with waiting customers.

"I'm staying here for the holiday," I said. "Mitzi and Colonel Draper are hosting us."

"In your own pub! That's a strange thing," Aggie said. "Well, I look forward to spending more time with you when it's quieter. Although when that'll be, I have no clue. If I don't see you before, I'll wish you a merry Christmas." She leaned over the bar and kissed my cheek.

"And to you." I looked down at the dogs. "I'll be back for them before the party ends."

"Don't worry about these two. They'll be as good as gold. I'll tuck them in the back room out of the way so they can get some shut-eye. They might like some pork scratchings, too."

"You're a Christmas angel," I said.

"Go on your way now," Aggie said. "Find a handsome young man to dance with and maybe have a cheeky kiss under the mistletoe."

I said a cheerful goodbye to Aggie and the dogs and headed back to join in the festive merriment. Although I'd keep a close eye on John if he was there. It appeared there was more to that unscrupulous chap than met the eye.

# Chapter 4

I awoke to a pale winter sunlight filtering through the lace curtains. For a moment, I was disoriented, mostly due to the faint pounding in my temples, but then the evening memories surfaced. I was at the Swan Tavern, having barely survived Mitzie and Eddie's lively party, charades, and champagne with Ruby until the early hours. We would have gone on until dawn if I hadn't insisted the dogs needed their beds. And so had I. A lavish party in one's thirties was a different beast than it was in my younger years. Perhaps Ruby had a point about us feeling our age.

I rubbed the sleep from my eyes and sat up, nudging Benji. He yawned, tail thumping. "Ready for breakfast, old chap?"

Benji softly barked an agreement. Tiberius seemed content to snuggle on the bed, so I fed him a biscuit, promised him a sausage when I returned, then dressed hastily, and we made our way downstairs, following the sounds of chatter and clinking china, to the private guest dining room.

Mitzie looked up from pouring coffee and beamed. She wore a beautiful cream cashmere sweater and fitted black trousers. "There you are! We thought you'd keep to your bed all day. Help yourself to kidneys and kedgeree."

I gratefully accepted a cup of strong coffee and filled my plate, joining Ruby at the table. Her eyes were also bleary, but she smiled. "Good morning. How's your head?"

"Tolerable. And yours?"

She groaned. "Ask me after three more cups of this heavenly brew."

Eddie grunted from behind his newspaper.

Mitzie tutted. "Really, Eddie, must you make that dreadful noise?"

He ignored her, rattling his paper to show exactly what he thought of small talk at the breakfast table.

Mitzie giggled. "Eddie is no longer a morning person now he doesn't have to get up with the bugle."

"We didn't use bugles during the war, my love."

"Well, harsh shouts from your commanding officer. All that is behind us now." She reached over and placed a kipper on his plate. "Peace and goodwill to all."

The priest I'd seen at the party last night ambled in, his round glasses askew. He greeted everyone as he helped himself to toast and potted shrimp, upending the entire dish onto his plate.

Mitzie made the introductions. "This is Father Bertie Bumble. He's our priest in Little Kennington, but he had to abandon ship when a pipe burst in the vicarage and his kitchen was flooded."

"Not just the kitchen. My office and the back parlour, too." Father Bumble had a low, warm rumble of a voice.

"Oh! Bad luck," Ruby said.

"Or good luck for me. Mrs Draper was a sport in offering me a room in the stable." Father Bumble joined us at the table. "I'm looking forward to Christmas with friends. I'm usually so busy that I rarely have time to pause and appreciate how glorious Christmas Day can be."

"We'll ensure you have a wonderful time," Mitzie said.

John slouched into the room a few moments later, dark circles under his eyes. He wore a pinstripe jacket over crisp trousers, and a green silk cravat. He didn't greet anyone, filling a plate and taking a seat, before pushing his food around and snapping when Mitzie's butler, Baxter, offered him coffee.

The final member of our party to arrive was the blond moustached man I'd noticed at last night's gathering. I'd been so busy enjoying myself with Ruby that I'd not spoken to him or been introduced. He was tall, sturdy, and had warmth in his blue eyes as he looked over the group.

"Devon! Don't stand on ceremony and collect a plate. It's serve yourself. Baxter isn't happy! He thinks I'm doing him out of a job." Mitzie gestured at the table, giggling at Baxter's impassive expression as he stood attentively by the coffee pot. "Then you must meet my two charming friends. They're spending Christmas here, too. Ladies, this is Devon Blaine."

We sat alert, and Ruby nudged me.

Mitzie spread jam on to her toast. "Devon, this is Veronica Vale and Ruby Smythe. And it's thanks to Veronica we have such a wonderful place to spend Christmas after our chilly old home let us down.

Wretched pipes. I shall never forgive the heating for failing when it was most needed."

Devon joined us with a small plate of breakfast. "Ladies, it's a pleasure. And this is your inn, Miss Vale?"

"Veronica, please. It's a family business. I'm not involved in running it, but I keep an eye on the profits and ensure the staff are happy. We have an excellent publican who runs the Swan. She's been here for years."

Mitzie smiled slyly, suggesting she sensed a matchmaking opportunity, but I was long past all that nonsense. "Veronica's late father made his fortune in the brewery business."

Devon nodded politely and accepted a coffee from Baxter with a quiet thanks.

I could have corrected Mitzie, but I sipped my coffee instead. Her version of how my family gained their wealth wasn't far from the truth. "What business are you in?"

"I'm a doctor of psychiatry. I've worked at Whittingham, Bethlem, and Hanwell. I follow the Ellis method."

Ruby tilted her head. "Is that pet therapy?"

His smile was indulgent. "Not quite. But how do you know about that? It's a specialist field of study."

"It's all thanks to Veronica. She's obsessed with animals. Didn't you take in a former furry resident from a psychiatric hospital?" Ruby asked me.

"Yes. A retriever. He's now having a fine old time of it in the countryside. Do your patients find the animal therapy useful?" I asked Devon.

"Absolutely! We champion humane treatment and meaningful work. Patients find comfort when caring for an animal. I find it gives them a purpose and takes their mind off of their troubles."

John smirked. "Some people are too damaged to be saved."

Devon's expression hardened. "I believe every man should get a second chance."

"What about a third? How many sob stories do you believe before you give up on a patient?" John muttered.

Mitzie clapped her hands together, breaking the tension. "No shop talk or banter! Now we're all here, who wants to go ice skating after breakfast? The pond in Poplar Park has been frozen for weeks, so it's safe. And I've had the skates sharpened. We can hire extras when we arrive at the park. I was just reading how much fun it is."

Ruby's eyes lit up. "Ice skating? What a treat! We knew you'd have us on the ice again before Christmas."

"I may sit this one out." I wasn't sure my feet would stand it after all the dancing in less than practical shoes.

"It'll be amusing. Please say you'll join us. We've had fresh snow overnight, so the park will be beautiful." Mitzie reached over and grasped my hand. "And the dogs will adore it."

I arched an eyebrow. "The dogs don't skate."

Mitzie laughed. "There's a first time for everything. What do you say, Benji?"

Benji nudged my hand, gazing up at me expectantly, although only because he wanted a sausage, rather than he was expressing his desire to see me flounder about on the ice. I sighed. I could never refuse such an adorable face. "Is it outdoors?"

"Absolutely! They tried one of those ghastly indoor rinks last year, but everyone complained. And why erect such a thing when there's a perfectly serviceable frozen pond?"

"Very well. But I can't promise how long I'll last before a hot cocoa and a sit down is required."

"I couldn't agree more. Baxter will bring the supplies. We can have a picnic on ice!" Mitzie gasped her delight. "And don't worry, they have an indoor seating area, so we won't freeze. How splendid."

Given Benji's longing looks and Mitzie's innocent joy, I couldn't help but feel a tingle of pleasure, too. I hadn't skated in almost a year.

After finishing breakfast, we headed to our rooms to find suitable clothing for skating. I changed into warmer boots, a borrowed skirt from Mitzie with a buttoned side seam for ease of movement, and added my trusty woollen coat. Then we left the Swan Tavern and made our way out of Ship Tavern Passage and on to Gracechurch Street. I had the dogs on their leads, although they rarely misbehaved, but with the London bustle around us, I didn't want them getting overwhelmed and bolting because something startled them.

The morning was clear but frosty. More snow had fallen, but the paths were salted, so the risk of slipping was minimal. The frozen pond was a brisk ten-minute walk away, and everyone agreed feet rather than wheels would be the safest mode of transport.

Father Bumble had brought a thermos of hot cocoa to drink along the way, although some of it ended up down his front as he walked, sipping it. He seemed happy, so I didn't want to embarrass him by pointing out the spillage.

The walk was bracing but enjoyable as we passed festively decorated shops, the air filled with the tantalising aroma of roasted chestnuts from street sellers. Through frost-kissed shop windows, I glimpsed displays of sparkling ornaments, luxurious fabrics, and toys waiting for a child to enjoy. Christmas was so close, I felt like I could reach out and grab it.

When we arrived at the ice, there were already morning skaters, but we were the largest party. Elegantly dressed ladies and gentlemen glided gracefully across the glistening ice, the park alive with the sound of blades carving into the frozen surface, punctuated by occasional laughter and muffled chatter.

Mitzie made sure everyone knew how to lace their skates before gliding expertly onto the ice. She spun and slid backwards, waving her arms. "Come on ladies, the ice is perfect!"

"Perfect for making a fool of myself, but I'm game." Ruby stepped out tentatively, wearing a warm felt hat and kid leather gloves, her skirts swirling around thick woollen stockings. "It's a shame Jacob isn't here to enjoy this. Although, perhaps the dashing Doctor Devon could keep you company instead," she teased.

"Jacob would hate this, and so would his leg. It's almost healed, but he still has a limp. I think it's permanent." I stepped onto the ice. "And as for the dashing doctor, you were the one who got perky when he joined us for breakfast."

Ruby smiled. "He is a handsome older man, don't you think?"

"I didn't notice." A foot slid out from under me, and I stopped to focus on my form.

Benji barked, as if to say 'you've got this,' while Tiberius looked confused by our shenanigans. I took a deep breath and slid one skate across the ice, then the other. I grabbed Ruby for balance, sending us both sprawling. Our laughter rang out across the ice, causing several skaters to slow and see what the kerfuffle was.

Eddie slid over, not wearing skates, and helped us up, grumbling under his breath. John zoomed over and offered his hand to Ruby. She waved him away with a polite rebuttal, linking arms with me instead, and we pushed off, slowly finding our balance.

Mitzie skated circles around us. "You've got it! Bend your knees and push. No, not like that!" She narrowly avoided colliding with Father Bumble, who was sliding about, his arms out.

We tried again, clutching at each other for balance as our skates slid and scraped. Benji suddenly appeared. He ran around us, barking excitedly.

"Benji! Off the ice," I instructed. "Be a good boy and sit with Tiberius."

"Benji is showing us up with his skating skills." Ruby laughed as Benji did a half turn, crouching onto his belly as his paws slid from under him. He soon decided the snow was the safest place and returned to Tiberius, who'd wisely remained by the edge of the ice with Eddie, man and dog staring at us with a mixture of disbelief and bemusement.

Ruby wobbled but soon got the hang of it, gliding forward with tentative strokes. "Look, I'm skating! It may have been a year since I donned blades, but you never forget once you pick up the technique."

Mitzie spun another circle around us. "You're naturals! Well done, ladies."

Father Bumble careened past at high speed, his cheeks ruddy from the cold and exertion. "Mind yourselves!" His cry faded as he careened towards the bank. He'd break a leg if he wasn't careful, but he was having fun.

The scrape of blades on ice and tinkles of laughter filled the air with a festive melody as I moved. My breath misted as I called to Benji to ensure he was happy. He barked in reply, dancing on the edge of the frozen water, but he was content to remain with Eddie and Tiberius.

John and Devon were also on the ice, but they'd stopped by the edge, some distance from Eddie, and were talking.

I felt much more chipper now I had the rush of icy air on my cheeks and my friends laughter surrounding me. I glided across the ice, and after several turns about the frozen surface, I almost believed I was a natural. I passed John and Devon again, who were deep in conversation. John ran a hand through his hair, his expression stormy. Devon's smile seemed strained.

Benji ran up to them, his tail wagging. Devon scratched him between his soft furry ears, but John ignored him. I slid closer, pretending to struggle with my skates and needing a moment to get my balance.

"...refuse to be involved, Robinson." Devon frowned. "You should never have asked me for help."

John snorted. "I can do this. It's a sure thing. Neither of us will lose. You've helped before, and I thought we were friends. I'd do the same for you if the situation was reversed."

"This will end badly, I warn you. Can't you find another way?"

"Like you? Make my money prattling pseudo-scientific nonsense about pets." John's top lip curled in contempt, and I felt a sting on Devon's behalf.

I glanced around, but I was the only one paying attention to the debate. The festive atmosphere seemed at odds with the tension between them.

Devon's eyes narrowed. "What I do is honest work. At least I don't gamble with other people's money, knowing it'll all go wrong."

I pretended to adjust my skates as I watched them. There was a flicker of something in John's expression—desperation, perhaps? His shoulders dropped ever so slightly before he straightened again.

"You don't understand." John's voice was so low I could barely hear. "This is my only option. One more helping hand, that's all I need to come good. Help a friend out at Christmas."

A heavy silence hung between them, broken only by the distant sounds of children laughing and skates scraping ice.

Devon sighed, a cloud of breath enveloping his face for a second. "There's always another way, John, so the answer is no. And it doesn't matter what time of year it is."

John's face hardened, the vulnerability vanishing as quickly as it had appeared. "Don't come crying to me when you realise you've missed out on the biggest opportunity of your life."

He yanked off his skates and strode away, his footsteps crunching on the snow-covered path that wound around the rink. Devon watched him go, resolve etched on his features.

I inhaled slowly, the cold air biting at my lungs. The encounter left an uneasy feeling in my stomach.

Devon caught me watching, and raised a hand before stepping off the ice, removing his skates, and walking away, too.

"Look out!"

A second later, I was on my back, Ruby squashing me. We slid apart, dazed.

"Oomph! So sorry. Are you hurt?" Ruby sat up, wincing and rubbing her elbow. "I went too fast and couldn't slow in time."

I rubbed my arm, surveying the damage. The back of my coat was soaked through. "No. That was my fault. I wasn't paying attention."

"What had you so interested? I thought you didn't have your eye on the handsome doctor?" Ruby wobbled to her feet.

"More like I had my eye on his argument with your Mr Robinson."

"John isn't mine. Not after you scared him off last night with your fierce looks and less-than-subtle comments. Not that I objected. He's not for me. I've been thinking about it, and I'm finished with relationships. As I found out the hard way, they only end in disappointment." Ruby helped me up and brushed ice off my coat. "What were they arguing about?"

"I'm unsure. I'd like to follow them, but Mitzie will wonder what's going on if we leave, and I don't want to spoil her fun." Mitzie was on the other side of the ice, chatting to a group of people, her gestures animated.

"Let's do another circuit," Ruby said. "They'll return, and then you can gently interrogate them about their disagreement."

I looked in the direction the two men had headed. "And if they don't?"

"We'll ply them with brandy later and ask what the fight was about. Some men can be stubborn. I expect it was nothing important."

"John wanted something, and Devon wasn't prepared to give it to him."

"Money? A job? The telephone number of an attractive friend?"

"I missed the start of their conversation."

Ruby grabbed my arm. "Let's not worry about those two hotheads. We're here for fun!"

We continued around the ice, then broke for refreshments an hour later, organised by the ever-loyal Baxter, who was bundled in a thick coat, but still looking the consummate professional.

The party had spent most of the time on the ice, but several times, people had stopped for a break or to take a walk around the park.

John and Devon hadn't returned, and the uneasy feeling niggled at me, so much so that I barely tasted the delicious slice of iced fruit cake I'd taken from the tray of delicacies Mitzie had provided. We hadn't managed to grab an indoor seating area, since they were all taken, and had to make do with chilly wooden benches, but I was warmed through after all the skating.

Mitzie dashed over, arm in arm with Eddie. "Jolly good! I was hoping we'd time our return when you were taking a break. I have a fancy for something sweet. Oh! Baxter. Did you take a tumble?" She helped herself to a slice of cake Baxter offered her.

"Unfortunately, I did, madam. I wasn't watching my step and slid over a short while ago when I was looking for suitable seating for you all." He sported a red welt on his forehead and one on the back of his hand.

"You poor dear. I should get you better boots if you're to be traipsing around in all this snow." Mitzie insisted he lean forward so she could inspect his head. "If you need the evening off, I'm certain we can look after ourselves. I may rely on you for everything, but I don't want you to suffer."

"Thank you. But I'm perfectly fine. The snow cushioned my fall."

After another half hour had slid past, with no sign of John or Devon returning, and with the threat of more snow looming, I found myself watching for their return. Had they continued their argument somewhere else? Then Devon suddenly strode up nonchalantly, brushing snow from his coat.

I jumped from my seat and accosted him. "Where have you been? You look frozen."

He appeared startled by my forthright nature. "I was taking a stroll. I wasn't in the mood for skating and decided to explore. I'm always so busy with my work that I rarely get time to look around London."

"And John? Did you explore together? I saw you leave at the same time."

Devon's expression darkened. "I don't have the faintest idea where he's gone. Although I think he's still drunk from last night."

"He seemed tetchy at breakfast. Did he say something to offend you when you were talking?" I asked.

Devon hesitated, then shook his head. "Nothing worth repeating. As I said, he can't hold his drink. It made him foolish."

"Your conversation was intense."

He lifted an eyebrow. "You overheard us?"

"No! Well, a few words. It was serious?"

"Nothing is ever serious with that man. Now, if you'll excuse me." Devon stalked off towards the main park exit, clearly having had enough of being grilled.

"Devon! Where are you off to now? Stay for hot cocoa." Mitzie waved at him, but he ignored her. "Veronica! What did you say to chase him away? I know how sharp-tongued you can be when a man doesn't live up to your high expectations."

Ruby chuckled. "There's nothing wrong with having exacting standards, although Veronica's are elaborate and multi-layered."

"Stuff and nonsense. He wasn't in the mood for convivial conversation." I settled back on the bench and finished my cocoa, but I struggled to relax.

Mitzie suggested another spin around the ice, but no one was keen. We were all cold and ready to get back and warm up in front of an open fire and eat a hearty late lunch, so we walked briskly back to the tavern.

"It looks like more snow is coming." Ruby pointed at the yellow clouds building on the horizon as we were almost at the end of our chilly walk.

"We don't need to worry about that," Mitzie said. "We'll soon be inside, warming by the fire, and can look forward to the festivities. Now, Veronica, why don't you tell me all about this delicious detective you've been so elusive over?"

I was glad my cheeks were already pink from the cold. "There's little to tell."

Ruby chortled. "Jacob Templeton is a catch. A slightly stuffy, emotionally tricky catch, but he's perfect for Veronica. And now they've stopped—"

"Thank you, Ruby. My personal life is just that." I speared her with a glare inspired by the icicles hanging from the gutters.

"Come now, you're among friends," Mitzi said. "Eddie, we should make Veronica tell us everything about her handsome catch, don't you think?"

"I know the fellow. It's a damn tragedy what happened to him, but Templeton is a solid chap. He'll make the best of things."

"Well, that's a ringing endorsement, and the best you'll get from my husband." Mitzi leaned in close. "I understand emotional stuffiness and how to fix it if you ever want tips in that department. Under Eddie's icy veneer lies the heart of a soft teddy bear."

I hid a smile behind a gloved hand. "I'll take that under consideration."

Benji lifted his nose in the air, and his ears lowered just before we reached the guest passageway leading to the Swan Tavern's side door.

I rested a hand on his head, recognising the signs he'd sniffed out something of interest.

Tiberius tipped back his head and howled. The sound was so eerie it made me shiver. Then both dogs took off, racing over piles of snow. I hurried after them, following their barks. I rounded the corner and stopped short.

Benji stood rigid, his hackles raised, growling at a prone figure in the snow. A very familiar figure. Tiberius joined in, but I gently silenced the dogs with a firm word. Although it was a tiny miracle how I was able to utter so much as a squeak.

The world around me seemed to slow the moment I saw him. John Robinson, lying crumpled on the ground. For a second, my brain refused to process what I was seeing. My body went cold, not the kind of cold that bites at your skin like a winter wind, but the kind that sinks deep into your bones, freezing you from the inside out.

A sharp, choking sensation rose in my chest, my breath coming out in shallow bursts as I stared at the smear of scarlet marring the snow around John's head.

# Chapter 5

Benji nudged John's body with his nose, whimpering as he did so. I stumbled over and dropped to my knees, heedless of the wet and cold seeping through my skirt. "Mr Robinson?" No response. Gently, I touched him to check for a pulse. There was nothing.

I leaped back when he moved. John was alive! Then he squeaked. No, it was more like a pained honk.

Benji whined and nosed at John's arm, and an orange beak appeared.

"What in the name of all things Christmas is going on?" I gently tilted John and gasped. He was on top of a small injured swan!

Mitzie's shriek pierced the air. I looked up to see her running towards us, one hand clutched to her chest, with Ruby, Eddie, Baxter, and Father Bumble in tow.

Eddie hurried over and immediately checked for a pulse. His expression tightened, and he shook his head.

"Help me to move him," I said. "There's a swan trapped underneath him."

"A ... good lord. So there is!" Eddie stared in disbelief at the surprising discovery. "What happened here?"

Mitzie peered over Eddie's shoulder. "Is John dead?"

I reached up and squeezed her arm, my heart racing. How had we gone from revelry to tragedy so swiftly? "John is gone, but the swan is alive. We must move John's body so we can help the injured animal."

Eddie bent at the waist and inspected John again. "We can roll him and get the swan out. Not that it'll be alive for long if John landed on it."

Father Bumble removed his glasses, polishing them with a handkerchief. "I know he wasn't a visitor to my church, but was he a Catholic? I can perform the last rites."

Mitzie shook her head. "I heard John say church was reserved for Christmas, weddings, and funerals, so I'm not sure the last rites would be suitable."

"Hurry! The swan." I assisted Eddie to twist John, revealing the small swan, one wing bent and her beautiful feathers flecked with blood.

"Oh! The poor creature." Ruby rushed forward, slowing when the swan hissed a warning.

"We'll put her in a shed. There are several farther back where the empty barrels are kept for collection. It'll be warmer in there, and she can get over the shock," I said. "I'll need a blanket to cover her head and wings. When she can't see us, she'll be less aggressive."

"We should put the creature out of its misery." Eddie stood back while Ruby dashed off to grab a blanket from inside the tavern.

"I've nursed injured birds before, and I'm not giving up on this one without trying everything I can to help her." I ignored Eddie's muttered comments about stubbornness. He knew me well enough to know I never abandoned an animal in need.

Benji nudged my hand. I rubbed his ears, trying to make sense of the scene. John Robinson, argumentative and too charming for his own good, but alive mere hours before, now lay dead in the snow outside my pub. Was this an accident or something more sinister?

Eddie sighed. "I'll summon the coppers. Baxter, find something to cover the body. The rest of you, get inside before you catch your death. There's nothing more we can do for Robinson."

Mitzie dabbed at her eyes. "The police? At Christmas?"

"A man is dead!" Eddie's expression softened, and he took her hand. "This won't wait on the season, my love. Let's do things by the book."

After Ruby had assisted me in moving the swan to a quiet, cosy storage shed, and we'd built her a nest of blankets, checked her wing, which thankfully wasn't broken, and left her food and water, we hurried into the tavern, bedraggled, frozen, and shaken.

I quickly changed into dry clothing, my mind turning over one thought. John Robinson was dead, and from the punishing wound on his head, I didn't think it was an accident.

I headed down to the guest sitting room in the pub and gazed at the company I planned to spend Christmas with. If John had been murdered, did one of them have blood on their hands? My immediate instinct pointed at Devon, who was nowhere to be seen. Only a few hours ago, he'd been arguing with John, and now John was dead. I wasn't a believer in coincidences, so Devon would be someone to speak to urgently. That's if he showed his face again. Perhaps he'd already fled the scene of the crime.

Ruby hurried over and clutched my arm. "What do you think? There was an awful lot of blood on the snow. An accident?"

"I don't believe so. We must keep our wits about us. Someone knows what happened to John, and I fear they may be in our party. We must find out what went on without spoiling the festivities for Mitzi."

Ruby drew in a breath just as Eddie marched into the room, his face stern. "The dratted telephone line is down. The snow must have damaged the line. It's a few miles trek to the station, but if I leave now, I can make it before it gets dark."

"You can't walk that far!" Mitzie dashed to his side. "Not with your leg. And it's already started snowing again."

Eddie peered out of the window and grunted. "Stop worrying. My leg is fine, and I've handled worse conditions than this."

"When you were younger, perhaps." Mitzie fussed over him.

"A storm is coming." Father Bumble was also looking out the window.

"It's already here," Ruby whispered to me.

"I'll march over. Get the coppers up to speed, and they can get this situation sorted," Eddie said.

Mitzie clutched her husband's arm. "Don't leave us!"

"It's safe, my dear. And they need to know what happened to John."

"Is it safe for us to remain here?" I asked loudly enough so the entire room heard, drawing their attention to me.

Eddie grunted again. "It's your pub, so you should know if it's safe or not. And this is a respectable part of London. I see no issue."

I arched an eyebrow. He must have realised what I meant, but he was being obstinate, most likely to avoid panicking Mitzi. Her nerves often troubled her, and with the stress of organising a last-minute Christmas gathering at an unfamiliar venue, she didn't need more trouble to fray her sensibilities.

"I'll try the line again. We'll have normal service shortly." Eddie hurried out of the room.

"Mitzie is worried, too," Ruby whispered. "Maybe she saw something. We should speak to her."

Father Bumble turned from the window and approached us. "Please, sit, my dears. Ladies shouldn't have to deal with such a troubling situation. You must be quite overcome by discovering Mr Robinson in such a dreadful condition."

"We've seen worse, unfortunately," I said.

"Oh, my. You have?"

"The war."

His mouth formed an O of surprise. "Ah! Of course. I understand."

I lowered my voice. "Father, what can you tell us about John?"

His eyebrows rose. "Very little. He was a new resident in Little Kennington, and unfortunately, not a man of faith. I invited him to my services on several occasions, but he sneered at the idea of worship. And as Mitzie confirmed, he was a lost sheep, but I tried to herd him towards the path of righteous worship."

"Did John have any enemies in the village?"

"Enemies! Not that I'm aware of." Father Bumble scrubbed at a small cocoa stain on his sleeve. "Why do you ask?"

I glanced at Ruby, and she nodded an encouragement. "I don't think John's death was an accident. Did you see the wound on his head?"

Father Bumble startled and drew back. "For a brief second. What else could it be? No, no, ladies. You must leave this to the authorities. This is not a subject for a gentlewoman to poke about in!"

"A man lies dead, and I don't intend to sit idly by while a killer roams free."

"Roams free! Killer! My dear lady, I enjoy a good book, but it seems you've read one too many detective stories. That head wound must have been from an accidental slip. The paths are treacherous at this time of year."

"I do enjoy reading, but we have experience in matters such as this." I kept my voice level. Father Bumble didn't know about our crime solving expertise.

He tilted his head. "I recall Mitzi telling me you wrote obituaries."

"Yes, among other things."

"That must make you brush close to death, but this is an entirely different matter." He patted my hand. "The police won't be idle when they learn of the situation."

"They won't know anything about it if the telephone line remains down."

Father Bumble clucked a noise with his tongue. "The Telephone Exchange is one of the most efficient services we have in this country. There will be men working on the repairs as we speak. Ah! Here's the Colonel. He'll have things ship shape in no time. Now, no more talk of murder. You don't want to alarm anybody."

Eddie frowned at me as he joined us. "Talking murder, Vale. Stop it. I know what you're doing."

I smiled sweetly. "I was simply engaging Father Bumble in a stimulating conversation about the telephone."

Eddie twitched his moustache and glanced at Mitzi, who was talking to Baxter. "You're a different cut of female, but this is a matter for the police. Until they arrive, I'm in command. And we'll say no more about murder."

"Did I say anything of the sort?"

Father Bumble cleared his throat, but made no move to correct me.

"My hearing is first rate." Eddie adjusted his shirt cuffs. "Gossip is beneath you. You're a smart woman, and know better than to spread untruths."

My cheeks flushed. "I'm not a harpy, spreading lies for entertainment. But you saw John's head wound."

Eddie tugged at his cuffs again. "I know John enjoyed a drink. He could have fallen and injured himself." His tone brooked no argument, but that didn't deter me. There had been red marks on John's face, and the blood in the snow suggested he'd met a violent end. I opened my mouth to protest, but Ruby squeezed my hand in silent warning.

"We should at least gather basic information about what everyone was doing and the last time we all saw John. It could help the police when they arrive. When will that be?" I forced my tone to sound neutral. This wouldn't be the first time I'd butted heads with Eddie, and the results were often fiery.

"I'll keep trying them on the telephone." He looked around the group and huffed out a breath. "Perhaps you're right. We may as well get things in order while everyone is here. Keep this business as efficient as possible."

"Almost everyone," I said. "Where is Devon?"

Eddie harrumphed. "He'll be back soon. He's reliable. Everyone, gather around. Baxter, refreshments for all, and a stiff brandy for me. Make it a large one."

"Me, too," Mitzie said. "Does anyone else need a medicinal tipple to settle their nerves after such a terrible shock?"

Father Bumble accepted the offer of a brandy, but I refused, preferring more hot cocoa and a clear head. Once we were settled in chairs, clutching cups of cocoa or glasses of brandy for warmth and comfort, the questioning began.

Eddie strode around, back ramrod straight, and fixed us each with a stern eye. "There's no cause for alarm, but while we wait for the police, I'll ask a few routine questions to clear up this incident." His gravelly voice was all military command.

"Perhaps we should do this in the morning?" Mitzi suggested. "Everyone is tired from the skating, and shock plays havoc with the digestion. I can already feel a bout of hiccups coming on."

"It's best to get this over with and ensure the police have everything they need. Then we can get back to why we're all here," Eddie said.

Mitzi huffed her unhappiness, but gestured for him to continue.

Eddie peered at Father Bumble. "Sir, you were on the ice with us. Was anything going on with John that had you concerned?"

Father Bumble looked stunned at being the first person questioned. "No! He didn't skate with me. And I was just telling Miss Vale and her companion that I didn't know him. He wasn't a churchgoer, despite my gentle suggestion he join my flock."

Eddie fixed me with an icy glare, already aware I'd been asking questions he believed were above my station. I remained resolute, returning his glare with a calm assertiveness. I may not have known John well, and what I knew of the man, I didn't appreciate, but he hadn't deserved such a cold and no doubt frightening death.

"You never saw the chap at the pub in Little Kennington?" Eddie asked Father Bumble.

He shook his head. "I rarely go to the pub. Drink doesn't sit right with me."

Despite the seriousness of the situation, I smiled behind my hand. Father Bumble had enjoyed plenty of alcohol last night, and was currently nursing a large brandy. I could just imagine him at the village pub, attempting to recruit more to his flock by downing an ale or two while sermonising on the state of the world.

The door to the guest sitting room opened, and Devon walked in, a light dusting of snow on his shoulders and in his hair. He stopped and looked around the group. "What-ho. It appears I've missed an impromptu party. Where was my invitation?"

When no one welcomed him in, his expression shifted to concern.

"This isn't a party," Ruby said softly.

"I can see that. Whatever the devil is wrong?"

I stood. "You didn't see John outside?"

"Why would I want to see him?" Devon shrugged off his coat and handed it to Baxter. "He's probably sleeping off a thick head. A rest might make him more even-tempered."

"There's no easy way to say this, but he's dead," Eddie said.

Devon's eyes widened. "Dead? But I only saw him a few hours ago. Is this some prank? If it is, it's in poor taste."

"Unfortunately, this isn't a prank. We found John when we returned from our skating," I said. "He was lying in the alleyway beside the tavern. You didn't pass him when you came in? We covered him, but ... well, you can still tell what's under there."

Devon turned to me, shock paling his face. "I had my head down and was in a hurry to get inside. It's snowing hard again. Good grief! He's really dead?"

I nodded. "A nasty head injury."

He staggered to a chair and slumped into it. "How did it happen? When?"

"I'm fact checking to learn what occurred," Eddie said. "I saw you talking to John at the park. What did he have to say for himself?"

I settled back into my seat as all attention went to Devon. He accepted a brandy from Baxter and downed it before speaking. "I ... I feel terrible. The last words

I said to the man were in anger. If I'd known this was about to happen to him..."

"What were those words?" I couldn't help myself from taking over the questioning.

Devon's eyebrows flashed up in surprise at my plain speaking. "It was a personal matter."

"The police will ask you the same question," Eddie said, making a point of not looking at me, although I could well imagine the frosty glare I'd receive if he did. "We may as well get it all out in the open."

Devon's throat bobbed. "It ... it was about a girl. Someone I didn't want John meddling with. He kept pressing for her information last night, but I laughed him off. I told him to come back when he was sober and serious about her."

"And he did?" Eddie asked.

"Unfortunately. I refused to divulge any information. It's not as if we knew each other well. Let's just say we didn't socialise in a professional or casual manner. And he never attended church, so there were few opportunities for us to become acquainted. I thought it was odd he approached me and demanded her information. Most unsporting. It was an uncomfortable conversation."

"John had a fancy for this woman?" I asked.

"Vale, if you please," Eddie said.

I murmured an apology I didn't mean, fussed with Benji's ears, and checked to see if Tiberius needed a biscuit. I was anxious to get to the truth. From what I'd heard, there'd been no mention of a girl. Perhaps they'd continued their argument away from the park, though, and events got out of hand. Maybe Devon pushed John and he fell, hitting his head. My mind spun out different scenarios, and I bit my tongue as I processed everything.

"If you could answer Veronica's question, I'd appreciate it," Eddie said. "Just to clear things up."

I exchanged an exasperated look with Ruby. Eddie was a stubborn old war horse.

"More like a fancy for her social standing, so I had no intention of helping him," Devon said.

I drew in a breath to ask where he'd gone when we'd all been skating, but Eddie got there first.

"You didn't skate for long," he said. "Where did you go after you left the ice?"

"I went for a walk. I was uncomfortable staying with John. He'd started to beg, and it was all rather embarrassing for both of us. I decided some distance would help him get a hold of himself."

"Very good." Eddie seemed satisfied with the quality of Devon's statement. I wasn't. "I know Veronica and Ruby were on the ice most of the morning. I had to help them up several times when they grew too ambitious with their speed. You must keep an eye on these high-spirited girls, so they don't get into too much mischief."

"How thoughtful of you," I murmured, while Ruby chuckled into her cup of hot cocoa.

"May I enquire as to why you wish to know my movements?" Devon asked. "What does it have to do with John's death?"

I opened my mouth, but Eddie beat me again.

"Most likely, nothing. We think he slipped on some ice," Eddie said. "It's the obvious conclusion."

"John's head injury suggests his death wasn't an accident," I stated.

"We don't know that for certain." Although Eddie's tone sounded less than robust. Was he having second thoughts about the accident theory?

"There was nothing on the ground John could have hit his head on," I said.

"You're not qualified to investigate, so no more gossip and speculation," Eddie said. "It's not helping this situation."

It was far from gossip. It was a well-founded suggestion, but I held my tongue again, to avoid rousing Eddie's fierce spirit. For how long I'd be able to do that, I was uncertain.

"Who found him?" Devon asked.

"Benji alerted us that something was wrong on our way back to the tavern," Ruby said.

Devon ran a hand through his hair. "There was no one with him?"

"He was alone," I said.

"We can rule out Father Bumble and Mitzie from committing any dark deeds—not that I believe anything untoward occurred—since they were skating, too," Eddie said.

"Father Bumble would never even think of committing such a sin," Mitzie said. "And neither would I."

"Quite right," Eddie said. "None of us are involved. Which convinces me even more this was an accident."

I made a show of looking at Devon. His alibi of going for a walk was flimsy at best. "We all left the ice at some point, to take comfort breaks or have some refreshments. Even Mitzie."

She squeaked. "Veronica! You can't think I was involved in such a dreadful thing."

"No, but I'm pointing out we were all absent from the ice during our skating trip. Father Bumble went to top up his cocoa and have a rest. Ruby got a sore foot and needed to change her skates. I had to—"

"Why look for complications?" Eddie snapped. "The man was a drunken cad. He was too full of self-confidence, and he missed his footing in the snow. We should stick with that theory until the police have tidied this matter and concluded the same."

"My love, remember, John is dead. Perhaps we shouldn't speak ill of him," Mitzi said.

I scowled. Eddie's basic line of questioning seemed designed to find no answers, and he had no intention of probing deeper into John's misfortune. As fond as I was of Eddie, he was accepting everyone's word at face value. We'd all left the ice, so technically, any of us could have attacked John.

"I'll go see about the telephone. The line should be working by now." Eddie headed off to try the telephone line again, and I could hold my tongue no longer. I followed him as he left the room.

"Do you mean to end your investigation there?" I asked.

"What investigation?" He continued his march along the hallway towards the telephone.

I steeled myself, knowing the barrage that awaited me if I continued, but I had defences strong enough to withstand Eddie's fiercest blast. "I've made no secret that I believe John's death wasn't an accident."

Eddie stopped and turned. "Vale, control yourself! I will not have you spreading hysteria with wild accusations. No one else is talking about murder."

My cheeks burned, but I refused to back down from his belligerent insistence that this was an accident. "You know me better than that. I never say ridiculous things. And better hysteria than allowing a murderer to walk free!"

He let out a sigh, his initial anger deflating. "We've both had a shock. It's not making us behave. My apologies for snapping. I've never seen you hysterical, not even under the most trying of circumstances."

I conceded. "I understand. But at least consider the idea."

Eddie let out a slow breath. "I knew John, you didn't. His character was murky. He was a drunk and a layabout. And ... this goes no further than us, but I told Mitzie not to invite him because it would lead to trouble, but she paid me no attention. She felt sorry for John because he'd be alone over Christmas. Just like one of your stray dogs, she couldn't abandon him."

"Mitzie is kind, so I'd expect nothing less from her," I said. "But I'm still puzzled as to how John died. Didn't you see the marks on his face? And if he fell, what did he hit to cause such a serious head wound?"

"He got those marks from a slip, trip, or a fall. It's all the same thing. And perhaps he fell somewhere else but dragged himself to the alleyway."

"A badly wounded man would have been seen. Half of London is out shopping! It must have happened when he reached the Swan Tavern. The alleyway is private, so no one would have seen a thing."

Eddie shook his head. "I told Mitzie it was too icy to take our guests out, but she didn't listen. Not that I blame her, but ... It's a damn shame. This puts a dampener on the whole thing."

"Then our Christmas will have to be damp! If the police can't get here, we must investigate."

His shoulders lifted. "There's nothing to investigate."

"I know you have doubts."

"I never doubt myself."

I tilted my head. "Eddie, we've known each other long enough to cut through the bluster. When you questioned Devon, you thought he was lying. He had a dispute with John, and now John is dead."

"He died from a fall!"

"Would you stake your reputation on that?" Eddie was a proud man who lived by a rigid code of rules.

He sighed. "The police will be here soon. The boys in blue won't let us down. And a little snow won't stop them from ensuring this is cleared up. I play cricket with most of them when they come out to Little Kennington. They're damn fine fellows."

"In case you haven't checked outside, a blizzard has rolled in. Much more of this bad weather, and we'll be trapped in the tavern. And potentially trapped in with whoever killed John. You don't want to put Mitzi at risk, do you?" I kept my voice low as the thought sent chills down my spine, but I kept my composure. I wasn't easily intimidated, especially not with Benji, Tiberius, and Ruby by my side.

"Even if something untoward occurred to John, and I'm not saying it did, I'll keep order and make sure no one loses their head. That includes you, Vale. Do we have an understanding?"

I clenched my hands, but hid them behind my back. "We both want the same thing."

"Exactly. Good girl. Now make yourself useful and ensure Mitzie doesn't become hysterical. Her nerves are fragile. I told her not to take on too much by hosting a Christmas gathering, but that woman is stubborner than I am." Eddie snorted gently. "I suppose that's why I adore her so much."

"I'll make sure Mitzie is fine. But what will you do?"

"Keep trying the police. The telephone line will soon be fixed. Now, no more talk of murder without having cold, hard facts." Eddie didn't wait for my reply, but strode towards the console in the entryway to pick up the telephone.

I didn't like going behind his back, but I wasn't sitting around waiting for the killer to be found. This wasn't my first brush with death, and I was happy to be accused of being a snoop if it meant justice was done. It was time to unmask the killer and ensure Christmas wasn't spoiled for everyone.

I returned to the sitting room, hiding my frustration at Eddie's stubbornness, but Ruby saw my vexation and hurried over to join me. "It didn't go well?"

"Eddie is as stubborn as a goat, but I don't blame him for behaving this way," I replied. "He doesn't want to upset Mitzie. Her nerves are on the fritz again."

"And while that's adorably sweet of him, neither of us believes John slipped and bumped his head, do we," Ruby said. "Did you see the marks on his wrists?"

"Exactly. Perhaps someone held him down," I said. "I got nothing out of Eddie, although I know he's considering the options, so I haven't lost all hope. While he ponders, I have an idea of where to get answers. We need to start with the eyes and ears of this family."

Ruby's expression brightened at the promise of the adventure to come. "We need to talk to Baxter!"

# Chapter 6

It took only a few moments to locate Baxter. He was going over the evening meal with the tavern's cook.

When we entered the downstairs parlour, Baxter rose to his feet, a look of restrained concern on his face at finding us there.

"May I be of service? Do you require additional refreshments?" His voice was polite and professional.

I nodded a greeting. "If you have a moment, Baxter, we'd like to talk to you in private."

He glanced at the cook, who looked on with interest, then led us back up the stone steps and into the main hallway of the tavern.

Since time wasn't on our side, I plunged straight into the questioning. "How well did you know John Robinson?"

If Baxter was startled by my questioning, he didn't show it. It was the sign of a true professional, having worked for the Draper family for many years, even returning to them after the war ended. "Mr Robinson was a new face in Little Kennington."

"How did he find himself at this party?"

"Mrs Draper is always welcoming to strangers, so she was quick to invite him to enjoy Christmas with the family."

"But how well did you know him?" Ruby asked.

"I knew his favourite drink was vermouth with a twist of lime, and he preferred red meat over fish. And he always enjoyed a full-bodied claret at dinner, and a cigar afterwards. Mrs Draper invited him to dinner three times to ensure he felt welcome in the village."

"But his character?" Ruby asked. "Did you like him?"

"It's not my job to like or dislike people who visit my employer," Baxter said calmly.

"Was John argumentative with anyone in Little Kennington?" I asked.

"Not that I witnessed, but my work keeps me busy, so I have few opportunities to visit the shops or socialise."

Ruby glanced at me, and I could imagine she was thinking about pulling out the thumbscrews to get more from our tight-lipped, polite butler, who answered questions without providing useful information.

"We're terribly concerned about what happened to John," I said. "And Mitzie has taken it badly. I know how loyal you are to the family, so you must want the best for them."

Baxter's serene demeanour faltered a fraction. "It was a shock for everyone. Perhaps I should bring more brandy? Or prepare Mrs Draper a sleeping draught?"

"No, that won't be necessary. But until the police arrive, we must be useful and find out more about John's character," I said.

There was a heartbeat of silence. "If you'll excuse me for asking, why would you do that?"

"Baxter, you've always struck me as a clever man, and you miss nothing that goes on in the manor house. You've always looked after us excellently every time we've visited," Ruby said.

"That's kind of you to say, Miss Smythe. It is my job to ensure everyone has what they need."

"And you also know how much we adore Mitzie and Eddie," I said. "So we must ensure their safety."

He drew in a sharp breath. "Do you have evidence to suggest they're in danger?"

"A body in the alley next to the tavern we're staying in isn't evidence enough for you?"

Baxter pressed his lips together. "It is a concern. But Colonel Draper isn't convinced of foul play, so why should you be?"

"Until we know for certain what happened, we're making it our job to find out if anyone was involved in John's untimely death," I said.

Baxter inhaled slowly. "Miss Vale, I'm aware of your reputation for winkling out information. And I've read a number of your excellent obituaries in the London Times. You have a talent with words."

"I enjoy the obituaries, too," Ruby said. "You learn so much about a person's life from what their family put in a death notice."

"Very true." Baxter's focus remained on me. "And I understand you served this country well during the war."

I nodded. "Ruby and I did our bit."

His gaze shifted to Ruby, and he dipped his chin. "Mrs Draper sometimes mentions you went above and beyond."

"Mitzie has a vivid imagination." Although it was possible, Eddie had let slip to her a few salient facts about our adventures during the Great War.

"I pay little attention to gossip, so I know you went beyond the requirements of any female to complete your missions. Well done. It's people like you who helped us secure victory."

"We did what was needed. And it's what we're doing now," I replied. "I need to make sure the family isn't at risk, and if there is a killer among us, he's brought to justice. The police still know nothing about this crime, so we must act while the evidence is fresh and memories crisp."

Baxter hesitated again, and his impenetrable mask cracked open as worry lines drew themselves across his forehead. "What do you have in mind to solve this mystery?"

"I've seen enough dead bodies to know what happened to John was no accident," I said. "I believe someone attacked him and left him for dead beside the tavern, and I intend to make sure that doesn't happen to anyone else in our party. We don't know the reason for this murder, so we can't rule it out as an isolated incident. Perhaps the killer has his sights set on someone else."

"Why would anyone target this party?"

"I don't know. That's why any information you may have about John could be crucial to solving this crime," I said. "Will you help us?"

Baxter drew back his shoulders, then gave an almost imperceptible nod. "Mr Robinson enjoyed a drink, and I saw him playing a few hands of cards at the village pub."

"He gambled with money?" I asked.

"Money changed hands."

"A lot?"

"Enough for a man who didn't have a steady job. And when Mr Robinson drank to excess, his sense of propriety dipped."

"John did things you didn't approve of?"

Baxter paused. "There were several occasions when I was concerned about his behaviour around Mrs Draper."

"Did he flirt with her?" Ruby asked.

Baxter nodded, his expression hardening.

I arched an eyebrow. "How did she respond?"

"Like a lady should," Baxter replied. "She was polite but firm in her rejection. I watched during their last encounter, and Mrs Draper made it clear she wasn't interested in Mr Robinson in any way romantic. She told him she considered him a friend but nothing more, and if he didn't mind his manners, she'd rescind his invitation to spend Christmas with them."

"How did John react to the rejection?" I asked.

"He was unhappy. He continued to press his attention on her until Mrs Draper suggested the use of her butter knife in a most inappropriate way." A smile flickered and died on Baxter's lips.

I held in my own smile, although Ruby was less discreet and chortled. "Good for her. Mitzie can always hold her own. I once saw her knee a—"

"Yes, that's enough," I interjected. "Mitzie is a loyal wife, and she adores Eddie, despite his curmudgeonly behaviour and grumbling. She'd never even think about straying, let alone act on such a thought."

"I won't comment on the Colonel's moods or behaviour," Baxter said. "He's a good employer, and I'm grateful for my job. And Mrs Draper is a most excellent lady, with a sterling character."

"Did John play cards with anyone while he was here?" Ruby asked. "Could he have got himself into financial difficulty and there was an argument?"

"It's impossible to say for certain. The times I saw him take part in card games, I didn't know the gentlemen he was associating with. Although I use that term loosely." Baxter glanced over our heads. "Let me just say, they wouldn't be the kind of chaps the Colonel would invite to supper."

"What do you know of John's background?" I asked.

"Nothing. I've spent barely any time with him. And when I have, it's been to provide him with refreshments, take his jacket, or show him to his room when he's stayed at the manor house after dinner."

"Do you know where he worked? Perhaps he had trouble there."

"I'm unsure if he had a job. The last place he mentioned was the meat processing factory in Stirling Row. Morbid and Poe, although he had nothing good to say about his employer," Baxter said.

"If you had to give an opinion of his character, how would you define it?"

Baxter looked over his shoulder. "Untrustworthy. I wouldn't be comfortable having my sister spend time alone with him."

"When did you last see John alive?" Ruby asked.

"During the skating in the park."

"He didn't skate for long, though," I said.

"No, but he was by the edge of the ice, talking to Doctor Blaine for some time."

"I saw John and Devon talking, too. Did you overhear their conversation?" I asked. "I only caught snippets."

"I never listen to private conversations."

I narrowed my gaze. "Are you sure about that?"

A dull flush spread up Baxter's neck and onto his cheeks. "Not when it concerns family business."

"Did the conversation between Devon and John involve the family?"

He smoothed a hand down his buttoned black jacket. "No. It sounded as if they'd made a deal, but something went wrong. It was something to do with money. I don't know what they were talking about, but Doctor Blaine was unhappy with something John had done."

I exchanged a pointed look with Ruby. That something had led to his murder.

"If you'll excuse me, I must return to my duties," Baxter said.

"Before you go, can you think of anyone else John had a problem with?" I asked.

"The only recent argument I can recall was with Doctor Blaine," Baxter said.

"What about less recent? Perhaps his gambling companions in the pub?"

Baxter shifted his weight, leaning back. "He locked horns with a local fellow in the village. Mr Nathan Dunmow. It was a clash of personalities, but I fear Mr Dunmow made an error of judgement by loaning Mr Robinson money."

"Nathan! He was in the main bar when I went in last night. What was he doing here if he lives in Little Kennington?"

"Hoping to see John and get his money back in time for Christmas," Ruby said. "He must have learned John was spending the holidays with the Drapers and confronted him."

"Nathan was furious," I said. "Aggie had to remind him of his manners."

"Maybe John made a habit of fleecing people," Ruby said. "He promised them a return on their loan, but then never delivered."

"It's a solid motive for murder," I said.

Baxter interrupted our discussion. "Ladies, while I'm grateful you're taking an interest in protecting the family, I must urge caution. If the killer, if there is one, learns of your involvement, he may not welcome your intrusion."

I waved away his comment. "We've dealt with scoundrels before. And this scoundrel has made the grievous error of interfering with my dear friends' perfect Christmas plans. That is unforgivable."

Ruby nodded. "Our gift to Mitzie will be to catch the killer. But who shall we start with?"

I considered our options. "We have Devon and Nathan as obvious suspects. I'll ask Aggie to look out for Nathan. She'll let me know the next time he stops by so we can have a friendly conversation. In the morning, we'll approach Devon, since he's already here, and find out why John spoiled his day on the ice. Was it over a lady friend or money?"

"Or something else? The possibilities are endless, but we mean to uncover them," Ruby said.

Baxter sighed. "Is there anything I can say to convince you to do otherwise?"

I gave him a conciliatory pat on the arm. "Sadly, not. But there's no need to worry. We're determined this murder won't spoil our wonderful Christmas."

# Chapter 7

I rose early the next day, after a poor night of sleep. I had the room next door to Ruby, so it was easy to sneak out and tap on her door so we could discuss the unfortunate dead body situation and how we planned on solving it.

Benji and Tiberius sat by my feet, while I sipped from the delicious cup of steaming coffee our new confidante, Baxter, had delivered to the bedroom, alongside a rack of fresh toast and marmalade.

"Ruby, you're perfect for this task," I said. "Your flirting skills sit in the advanced combat range."

"I'm happy to unleash my feminine wiles if I must," Ruby said on a theatrically dramatic sigh, "but I'd rather use strong-arm tactics to get the truth out of Devon about his dealings with John."

"You may have to if he gets feisty. But I came on too strong yesterday when I confronted Devon about the argument. Direct questions aren't favoured by him. Eyelash fluttering may be the way to go. Men bend to flattery. It disarms them."

"I'm well aware what a shapely calf and a sweet smile can do to a man, but I vote for tying him to a chair, and getting a confession," Ruby said. "And why must it be me who flirts?"

"You know full well my flirting abilities are a touch stiff."

"Unless it's a dog! You go gooey over a cute puppy."

I reached down and patted Tiberius and Benji. "How can one not? And I'm most excited about the Christmas event at the dogs' home. I hope we can get there. The snow has been coming down all night."

"My skills on the road outmatch any snowstorm." Ruby munched on a piece of toast. "You should be the flirt. This is a chance to improve your skills."

"And risk the mission going awry? You capture all the men's attention."

Ruby gave a less than gentle snort. "You're the siren!"

"Not when that siren is covered in dog fur and has a pocket bulging with meat flavoured chews."

Benji lifted his head at the sound of one of his favourite words and thumped his tail on the floor, ever hopeful of a treat.

"As you always say, 'love me, love my dog.'" Ruby arched her eyebrows. "Although, have you ever considered that's why it's taken you so long to snare a man?"

I pinched her arm. "No one should ever set out to snare anything. Man or hare. My time as a single woman was out of choice. And I haven't always been single. Technically, you could say I'm off the market now. According to my mother, I'll be prancing along the aisle by springtime. She keeps asking when Jacob will propose. As if we're anywhere near that prospect."

"Wouldn't that be delightful." Ruby set down her toast crust. "Did you manage to reach Jacob on the telephone?"

"No. It's such a nuisance. The line is still faulty. He must be wondering what's going on."

"He knows you're here, and I'm sure he's checked the weather, so he'll be aware London is trapped inside a snow globe."

"Yes, I'm sure you're right." I wanted desperately to speak with him, though, and learn of his progress as he investigated the mystery surrounding my father's death.

"Will you want me to be a bridesmaid?" Ruby asked. "I should warn you, spring is a busy time for me."

"I didn't know you had your calendar of social events planned so far in advance."

She looked away. "I mean with work. Lady M wants to expand her stud numbers, so we'll have foals in the stables."

"You don't look after the little ones, though. You ride and deal with Lady M's correspondence, so the foals won't bother you."

Ruby sighed. "I just want to make sure I'm available to be the most splendid bridesmaid."

"If, and this is a giant if, I ever decide to marry, I'll give you plenty of notice. And I assure you, it won't be for at least five years. Maybe even ten."

"You'll be grey-haired and stooped over if you wait that long!"

"I'll be a mature, level-headed woman who knows she's doing the right thing."

"You're such a romantic clod."

That comment earned her another pinch. "I'm a sensible clod. Now, finish your toast. Then we have a killer to catch."

"A part of me hopes Devon is innocent. He's not a bad-looking chap, and pickings are slim since the war." Ruby slid off the bed to dress.

"Are you serious about getting involved with someone after what happened in Margate? You told me you were done with relationships."

Ruby disappeared into the bathroom I shared with her. "You can say his name, you know. I won't vanish in a puff of misery smoke and tears."

I had been tiptoeing around the whole Alfonso leaving Ruby at the registry office debacle. His interference had threatened our friendship, and that was unforgiveable. "Have you heard from your Italian Lothario?"

"Not a peep. And I didn't give him my address, so he has no way of contacting me."

I hesitated, then ploughed on. "Would you like him to reach out to you and make amends?"

"And let him charm and deceive me again? Not on your nelly." Ruby came out of the bathroom and stood in front of me, so I could button the back of her dress. "Oomph. I shouldn't have eaten such a big dinner."

"The snug fit is due to too many Christmas treats. You can blame my mother. Every time you visit, she insists you take something with you. Last time, it was a whole tin of mince pies. And I know you ate them all to yourself."

"I gave one to you! You'll only hear me complain about the delicious food when I have to buy new clothes. Although I adore shopping, so the only thing that'll be sad is my purse." Ruby exhaled as I forced the final button into place. "That's got it. Shallow breaths only for me today."

"So we won't be chasing Devon if he makes a run for it when we question him?"

She chuckled. "We'll let Benji and Tiberius do the running, shall we?"

Benji lifted his head and wagged his tail. He was always happy to go for a run.

"It's time to put your flirting skills to the test," I said to Ruby.

"Oh, if we must." Her reluctance was feigned. Even after all her heartache, Ruby loved nothing more than a good flirt with a handsome fellow. "But I smell kippers downstairs. We can have a second breakfast before we sleuth."

"No kippers for you, or you'll waft fishy breath over our target, and that will ruin the romantic ruse."

"Love me, love my fishy breath," Ruby quipped. "Maybe Baxter will save me a kipper. We could have a fishy brunch."

I wrinkled my nose. "Sounds divine. But first, we cast our net and catch our killer."

After I'd made myself presentable and given Benji and Tiberius their breakfast and a quick run in the fresh, deep snow, we searched the tavern for Devon. But there was no sign of him.

"We should send the hunting dogs after him." Ruby nodded at Benji and Tiberius, who'd been following us like faithful shadows. "I've knocked on Devon's door several times, and he hasn't answered. Do you think he's fled? He could be afraid we're closing in on him."

"Devon has no idea we consider him a suspect, so he has no reason to run. And it would be a foolish move to flee while questions are being asked," I said.

"We can't be the only ones wondering if he followed up the argument with something more final." Ruby pressed her hand against her chest. "He could have chased after John and whacked him on the head."

"If Devon is innocent, he'll stay and defend himself," I said. "Let's gather the evidence before we send sweet Benji and innocent Tiberius on the hunt. Besides, they're lovers, not fighters, especially Tiberius."

To prove that point, Benji rolled onto his side and exposed his belly for a tickle. Tiberius quickly followed him, exposing a pink belly with adorable brown freckles on the skin. Of course, I couldn't resist giving them a scratch.

Ruby rested her hands on her hips. "If Devon doesn't make an appearance soon, we'll have to put his name forward to the police, should they ever arrive."

"Who's that you're talking about?" Eddie came down the main staircase, limping slightly.

"Good morning," I said. "We were looking for Devon."

He harrumphed. "Why would that be? Not snooping, I hope?"

I had the decency to blush at being caught. "Is there any word from the police?"

"There's still no working line."

"Drat. I was supposed to telephone Jacob yesterday and see how things are going."

"What is he helping you with? The last I heard, Templeton was jobless after that business with the bomb," Eddie said.

I bit my tongue, annoyed by my thoughtless comment. No one knew Jacob was on a clandestine mission involving my father's cold case. "We're working together. We should have an office open in Kent soon."

"Oh! I didn't know you already had a case," Ruby said. "Why didn't you tell me?"

"It's more of a personal matter. Jacob has the right contacts, so I'm letting him take the lead."

Ruby narrowed her eyes, sensing I wasn't being fully transparent, but she didn't press for more information.

"Bad luck, old girl. With the heavy snow overnight, I doubt the telephone line will be working today." Eddie inhaled as if preparing to lecture us on our unladylike snooping, when the private guest side door to the tavern was shoved open and a snowy figure hurried inside.

It was Devon! Barely recognisable until he unwound his red woollen scarf and removed his hat. I shot my most innocent smile at Eddie, who gave a disgruntled snort, then limped off, no doubt to find breakfast and complain to Mitzie we were misbehaving again.

Ruby winked at me. "Devon! You must be frozen through. What were you doing out so early?"

He looked a trifle startled by her overly enthusiastic greeting, but smiled as she took his hat and brushed snow off it. "I needed a walk. I didn't get a wink of sleep thinking about John."

"Of course. It's such an awful business. Would you like a drink to calm your nerves?"

He glanced at the gently ticking clock on the wall. "It's not even nine o'clock in the morning."

"For medicinal purposes. I'm sure you've given brandy to patients when they're in shock."

"Not recently." Devon smiled, but shook his head. "I would like a coffee, though."

"Right this way." Ruby took his arm and led him into the sitting room before calling Baxter and requesting coffee for all of us.

I acknowledged Devon and followed them, but I made a point of not joining the conversation and took a turn around the room with the dogs, inspecting the book shelves, admiring the festive garland, and appreciating the warmth from the crackling open fire.

"It's a shame the festivities have to come to such an abrupt end," Ruby said to Devon.

"What do you mean?" He settled in a high-backed winged armchair. "What's been cancelled?"

"Well, with what happened to John, I don't expect anyone is in the mood to celebrate. Mitzie is so disappointed. She works hard to ensure everyone has fun, and she was looking forward to Christmas."

Devon steepled his fingers. "We can't put Christmas on pause because John got himself into trouble. It was only a matter of time before something like this happened to him."

Ruby glanced at me, and I pretended to busy myself by admiring a watercolour painting on the wall. "You didn't care for him?"

"I can't say I did. And I didn't know he'd be in this party. But I shouldn't have been surprised. Mitzie loves to pick up the village's waifs and strays."

Ruby gently rested a hand on Devon's arm. "I hope you don't think I'm prying, but I saw you arguing with John at the park. It looked serious."

"Aren't arguments always serious?"

"Oh! Well, this one looked particularly grave. Did he say something to offend you?"

Devon sat forward in his seat. "You've experienced John's particular brand of charm after spending time together."

Her cheeks flushed. "John was entertaining, although his flattery seemed hollow."

Devon grimaced. "When John saw a pretty target, he went after it, regardless of her availability."

"You mentioned you were fighting over a woman," Ruby said.

"It was barely a fight, but I warned him away from meddling with a very close friend. She's worth more than that deceitful cad could ever offer her."

"Deceitful? What has John deceived you about?" Ruby asked.

I turned away from the books, interested in hearing the answer.

Devon shrugged. "It was always hard to know if anything he said was true. There may have been a kernel of reality in some of his tales, but he'd embellish to impress, usually a woman. And if they were wealthy, even more so."

"You make him out to be a terror," Ruby said. "John was too falsely charming for my taste, but I sensed nothing deviant in his nature."

"Then you were fortunate. And you had your friend watching out for you." Devon nodded at me. "If you'd been alone, John would have been much more persistent and grown increasingly less friendly as you refused him. And he'd been drinking, which made him even more of a problem. Some men shouldn't indulge if they can't keep control of their sensibilities."

"It sounds as if you've had several run-ins with him, since you know his character so well," Ruby said.

"Our paths have crossed from time to time. More's the pity. I live in Little Kennington, too, and it's such a small place. Everybody knows everybody else's business. And an eligible bachelor like John became the talk of the village as soon as he arrived. He relished that vaunted position and took advantage of his novelty."

I didn't miss the sarcasm and possibly jealous notes in Devon's tone.

Ruby touched Devon's arm again. "I can't think why anyone would consider him so eligible. You were the most handsome man at the party."

A smile traced across his mouth. "And now the most alive. That gives me a distinct advantage."

"Well, I suppose it does!" Ruby looked at a loss as to what to say next, so I nudged Benji into action and sent him over to join in the conversation. Anyone of good character would always welcome him.

"Benji, come back! They don't want to be disturbed." I hurried over, pretending to bring my disorderly dog under control. Tiberius wasn't so well trained and lurked behind me, always nervous when dealing with a new acquaintance.

"He's fine." Devon patted Benji.

"Did you see John after your debate at the park?" I asked Devon.

"I'm happy to say I didn't. We went our separate ways, and I was content for things to remain so."

"You really didn't like him, did you?"

Devon let out a sigh, absently scratching behind Benji's ears. "When John first came to the village, I made the mistake of spending an evening in the pub with him. I decided not to do that again."

"Why not?" Ruby asked.

"For the reasons I've already told you. We all did our bit during the war, but the way John told things, he single-handedly saved us from the central powers. Solved the whole blethering war and drew up the surrender documents himself."

"You served?" I asked.

"In a manner of speaking. I have a protected occupation, but I've been working with soldiers to deal with their trauma. And I'm sad to say, my diary has been full ever since those left standing returned home."

"The war took its toll on many," I said. "Facing constant stress, danger, and uncertainty isn't something you snap out of. My brother, Matthew, served, and he's had trouble ever since."

Devon nodded, his expression curious. "I heard from Mitzie you ladies helped out. Admin work, was it?"

"Something like that," Ruby said sweetly. "Of course, nothing as valuable as your occupation. Our boys need all the help they can get now they're no longer in the trenches."

"The problem is they're not getting enough help, and there aren't enough qualified people to support them, so I only see the most desperate of cases." Devon shook his head. "It's why I got angry when John belittled my work and then bragged about everything he'd supposedly done to secure our victory."

"Some of it could have been true," I said.

"I'm not sure John was even on active duty during the war. At least, not for long," Devon said. "When I queried him about his more outlandish comments and the places he was stationed, his answers became vague, and he quickly changed the subject whenever I mentioned anything specific to his unit or service record."

"John did the same with me," Ruby said. "I assumed he wanted to keep the party light-hearted and not get into deep conversation, but perhaps he was concealing a lie and didn't want to get caught out."

Devon sank back into his seat and sighed. "All I wanted was to attend a fun Christmas gathering and take some much-needed time off from work. Now, I find myself in the middle of this problem."

"Your work does sound stressful," I said.

"I rarely have time off. I'm thinking this was a mistake, though. I should have stayed at home and had a Christmas dinner for one. I'd have gone to the pub, but it's closed because of burst pipes. This deep freeze isn't doing us any favours."

"That would have been a miserable Christmas," Ruby said.

"Or I could have worked. There's always something to keep me busy."

"Do you know where John worked?" I asked. "They'll need to be informed about what happened to him."

"He didn't have a job. He mentioned leaving his last place, some meat factory near here, after an argument with his employer. I wasn't surprised. John wasn't the most reliable of men." Devon sighed. "I hope the police arrive soon and put the matter to rest. I'm fond of the Drapers, so I don't want this to spoil their plans."

"The police will be here as soon as they can," I said. "I didn't see you on the ice after your disagreement with John. Did you go somewhere fun? I don't know this part of London well."

"I didn't visit anywhere in particular. In the end, I walked back here and rested. I wasn't in the mood to be sociable, and I didn't want to snap at anyone who didn't deserve it. Mitzie would have been mortified if she knew I wasn't enjoying myself. I know she suffers with her nerves."

"You were alone?" Ruby asked.

"Unfortunately, I didn't have your charming company to entertain me." Devon's smile was rueful.

She smiled back. "Well, we shall have to make up for that."

"There you are, Blaine." Eddie entered the room, still wiping his moustache, suggesting he'd eaten his breakfast at double speed. "I'm sure the ladies can do without you now. I've got a few questions. Let's take this to the billiard room, shall we?"

"I'm happy to oblige, Colonel." Devon stood. "Ladies, if you'll excuse me, I'll see you at dinner, if not before."

"We're looking forward to it." Ruby waited until Devon left the room before turning to me. "He's got no alibi! And he came back to the Swan Tavern. He also made no attempt to conceal his dislike of John. Could we have our man?"

"We'll have to check to see if anyone saw him returning here alone."

"He could have waited outside for John and attacked him in the alleyway."

Without an alibi and having recently argued with our victim, Devon had to be our prime suspect.

A flicker of excitement danced in me. "You could be right. Now, all we need is evidence or a confession of his guilt, and we'll wrap up this murder."

"And top it with a ribbon!" Ruby smiled. "I do so enjoy it when the mysteries are simple to solve."

My smile wavered. So did I. But were we being a touch speedy in focusing only on Devon?

It was time to learn more about Mr John Robinson.

# Chapter 8

"This smell is doing nothing to settle my sensitive stomach." Ruby pressed a gloved hand against her middle.

I had to admit, it wasn't the most pleasant of smells. But then, a meat processing factory would never smell fragrant. "I expect all those martinis aren't helping."

"I barely had any last night," Ruby said. "I wasn't in the mood."

"You're always in the mood for martinis. Perhaps you're coming down with something."

"Don't say that! I refuse to be unwell over Christmas," Ruby said. "Why can't we be gift shopping, like you said we'd be doing to Baxter, rather than this?"

"If we have time, we can browse on our way back to the tavern, but I had to come up with a suitable reason for our hasty exit. Eddie would have blown a gasket if I'd told him we were still snooping."

"He'll blow a gasket knowing we're out and didn't stop at a police station to let them know about John. How will we explain that?"

"Once the police become involved, we'll be shoved aside," I said. "We need more time to figure out what happened. They'll be eager to close the case swiftly and continue their Christmas celebrations."

"John may not have been an upstanding citizen, but he deserves an answer to his untimely death."

"Exactly. With a bit of luck, Eddie won't notice us missing," I said.

"And even if he does, I can say we just went for a short spin, but it was too dangerous."

"Yes! We wanted to shop, but you lost control and your nerve, so we retreated."

"As if I'd ever do such a ghastly thing. If he does yell at us, at least we have afternoon tea to look forward to when we return," Ruby said.

"Father Bumble seemed most excited to accept an invitation to join us. I noticed he enjoys anything sweet, so I assumed he'd not be able to resist indulging in a scone and jam while we gently question him."

Ruby pressed her lips together. "Let's get this over with. But I'll need a bath later to remove the smell from my hair."

The sign outside the factory we'd carefully driven to read Morbid and Poe Meat Company. This was our victim's last known place of work.

"May I help you, ladies?" An efficient-looking woman wearing a pair of horn-rimmed glasses appeared behind us while we stood outside the factory. "If you're waiting for your husbands, the shift doesn't end for another half an hour. I suggest you go down the road to the local café. They do a nice iced bun, and their tea is strong enough to stand a spoon in."

"Perhaps later," I said, and made the introductions. "We were hoping to meet with Mr Blackstone. He's the factory owner, is that correct?"

"He runs the meat processing, if that's what you mean," the lady said. "I'm Miss Wright. I help him with the paperwork."

"Does the unique factory smell linger in your office?" Ruby asked.

"I can't say as I notice any smell," Miss Wright said. "You get used to it after a while."

I speared Ruby with a warning glance. There was no reason to get on Miss Wright's bad side before we'd even begun. "Would it be possible to see Mr Blackstone now?"

"The last time I checked on him, he had his feet up in the office. He's already enjoying Christmas, if you know what I mean." She made a drinking motion with one hand.

"Everyone is getting into the festive spirit," I said.

"I wish I could, but the mean old bugger won't let any of us leave early on Christmas Eve. He quoted some nonsense from that book with Scrooge in it. He claimed old Scrooge wasn't going to let his assistant have Christmas Day off! If he tried that with us, we'd walk out, leaving him to look after his own lumps of meat. Still, I can't complain. We all get to take home a hamper of steak and mince, so I won't have to worry about what to cook on Christmas Day."

"Is that so?" An idea formed, one which I hoped I'd be able to tackle before leaving the factory.

Miss Wright nodded. "Follow me. If he's not too merry, I'm sure he'll welcome two pretty faces. It's all men working in the factory these days, so I'll take you through the back way. They don't know how to behave themselves, and no one wants to hear all their hollering and wolf-whistling."

"If anybody causes us trouble, we know how to handle ourselves," I said.

Miss Wright snorted a laugh. "I should enjoy seeing that. I've had to clip a few around the ears. Most of them behave, but there are always some who leave their manners in the gutter." She led us around the side of the warehouse, through a small entrance, and into a bare corridor with the occasional crate standing empty. The smell of raw meat grew intense as we passed several large metal sliding doors.

Ruby pressed a hand to her mouth, her skin alarmingly pale. Although the smell was strong, it wasn't dreadful. Just pungent. I rifled around in my handbag until I found a small crumpled bag of peppermints and passed them to her, which she gratefully took and popped one into her mouth.

"Take a seat in the corridor, ladies. I need to put this paperwork on my desk and then I'll rouse the lazy old thing." Miss Wright disappeared behind an opaque glass door, and I sat with Ruby for several minutes as we sucked peppermints and breathed shallowly.

"I'm jolly glad I never worked in a place like this during the war," Ruby said. "I'd feel constantly unwell. The men must have cast-iron stomachs."

"Or no sense of smell," I said. "And as Miss Wright mentioned, you get used to it."

"There are some things one's nose should never get used to," Ruby said.

"You may have to bear with it for a short while longer," I said. "I have an idea, but I'll need your help."

Ruby narrowed her eyes. "Just so long as it doesn't involve me and meat, I don't mind what your idea is."

I tilted my head from side to side. "You'll change your mind when you know the reasoning."

Miss Wright returned before Ruby could question me further. "Mr Blackstone will see you now. He was interested in why two ladies are visiting his factory. I should warn you, there's half a bottle of whisky on his desk, which he's been dipping into all morning. If he causes you any nonsense, you shout for me. Although, I don't think he will. He's a decent sort, if miserly."

A few moments later, Ruby and I were settled on the opposite side of a shabby desk. It was a tidy desk, no doubt thanks to Miss Wright's excellent handiwork. There was a pile of paperwork in front of Mr Blackstone, a pen, his whisky, and an ashtray.

Mr Blackstone was a corpulent man dressed in a three-piece grey suit with a red tie. He had a few wisps of greying hair combed over his bald head, and a large bushy beard.

"This is a rare treat," he said after he'd shaken our hands. "I know my workers' lady friends by sight, so you're not with anyone in the factory. What brings you to my door?"

"We have a question about a former employee and wondered if you could assist us," I said.

"I keep excellent records. Well, Miss Wright does. Truth be told, she runs this place, although you'll never hear me say that to the men. I'd be a laughingstock."

"It is remarkable what a woman can do when given an opportunity," I said.

"I couldn't agree more," Mr Blackstone said. "I have four daughters. Four! They're all headstrong and too clever for their own good. One of them is in Spain on her own. She's a teacher. She heard about a programme for young single ladies to get themselves a continental education and put herself forward without my permission. After I'd yelled at her, I realised how proud I was. If the war taught us anything, it's that we underestimate the fairer sex. When all my men went to serve, the women kept this place going."

"It's a pleasure to meet a man with such an open mind," I said.

"There are few of us about, but I'm proud to be one of them." Mr Blackstone regarded us levelly. "Before I answer any of your questions about my employees, former or current, I have to know why you're interested. This chap's not got either of you into trouble, has he?"

"It's nothing like that," I said. "Unfortunately, this former employee is dead. Possibly murdered. We were told he used to work here, so we're looking into what happened to him. He died in the alley beside my pub."

Mr Blackstone jerked upright in his chair, almost knocking over his glass. "Dead! Who are we talking about?"

"John Robinson." I waited for a reaction, but Mr Blackstone didn't flinch. "We understand he'd been let go from his position not so long ago."

He settled back into his chair, his fingers drumming on the edge of the desk. "I remember him. He wasn't a model employee."

"What can you tell us about him?" I kept my tone carefully neutral.

"John was a decent enough worker, but he started slipping. Coming in late, leaving early. Then I caught him with his hand in the till, so to speak. Pinching stock when he thought no one was looking."

"What was he taking?" Ruby's voice was steady despite the lingering smell that had made her so queasy.

"Meat," Mr Blackstone said. "Not just scraps, either. Prime cuts. I'd noticed the books weren't balancing. My security man caught him. John denied it, of course, but we found the proof in his bag."

"So you let him go?" My gaze fixed on his as I read the emotion crossing his face. He didn't appear nervous, simply stating facts.

"I had to. I couldn't have him setting a bad example for the others." Mr Blackstone sighed, running a hand over his face and tweaking his beard with his fingers. "I might have been willing to let it go if it was a one off, give John a warning, but when I confronted him, he got mean. We nearly came to blows, and some of the lads had to haul him away until he calmed down."

I exchanged a glance with Ruby. "When did this happen?"

"About a month ago. John went off in a rage after that, muttering about how he'd make me pay."

"Did you see him again after your disagreement?" I asked.

Mr Blackstone shook his head. "And a good job, too. This is a respectable place. We don't need troublemakers stirring things up. Now, I have a question for you."

"Go ahead," I said.

"I'm not a stupid man. If you're asking these questions, you must have concerns. Are they about me?"

"John's injuries weren't self-inflicted, nor caused by an accident." I left the rest unsaid.

Mr Blackstone exhaled slowly. "I didn't think much of the fellow, but John was no longer my problem. And it wouldn't be the first time I've had to let someone go because they couldn't keep their hands off the stock. You'll be glad to know they're all still alive."

"If you don't mind me asking, where were you yesterday, in the afternoon?"

Mr Blackstone's eyebrows flashed up. "You're seeking my alibi?"

"I own the pub where John died, so I must protect my business interests. I'm sure you understand why I'm pressing for this information."

He huffed out a breath. "I suppose so. Well, I was here. Ask Miss Wright. She knows my diary better than I do."

"I believe you," I said. "You're most fortunate to have her."

"And well I know it." Mr Blackstone offered us cigarettes, and then lit one for himself. "Even though we argued, I didn't lay a finger on the man. Whatever trouble John got himself into after leaving here, it has nothing to do with me."

"Was John the type to hold a grudge?" Ruby asked.

"Like you wouldn't believe," Mr Blackstone said. "He had a chip on his shoulder the size of a boulder. And he always thought the world owed him something."

"Did he have any friends at the factory who may be able to help us?" I asked.

"He kept to himself," Mr Blackstone said with a shrug. "But there was one bloke—Kevin. They used to sneak off together during breaks. They talked a lot, though about what I couldn't tell you. Kevin is still on the payroll, so he might know more."

I nodded, making a mental note to speak with this Kevin. "Thank you. You've been very helpful. We appreciate your time."

Mr Blackstone stood to show us out. "I hope you learn what happened. I didn't think much of the man, but it's a rotten way to go. Have a good Christmas, ladies." He pointed to the mistletoe outside his door, and Ruby obliged him with a kiss on the cheek. I shook his hand.

"Do you think he was hiding anything from us?" Ruby asked once the door was closed and we were alone in the corridor.

"I don't think so. We need to check with Miss Wright to confirm he was here. And we need to find John's friend, Kevin, and see what he knows. After that, we have a favour to ask."

"What's the favour, and who are we asking?"

"Did you see the photograph of that magnificent deerhound when we passed Miss Wright's desk?"

Ruby appeared perplexed. "I can't say I did. Veronica, what scheme have you come up with?"

"A tiny Christmas miracle, but a big one for the dogs' home. They deserve a Christmas luncheon just as much as we do. Follow me."

Ruby wrinkled her nose. "Does this miracle have to do with what this factory processes?"

"Oh, my! You're clever and pretty. That's a dangerous combination."

"Flattery won't work if you expect me to go anywhere near lumps of uncooked meat."

I linked arms with her as we returned to find Miss Wright. The door to her office was slightly ajar, and I could see her sitting at a desk, her fingers flying over the typewriter keys with practiced ease. On the corner of her desk, a small framed photograph of a handsome deerhound sat.

I knocked lightly, and Miss Wright looked up, her stern expression softening into a smile as she saw us.

She removed her glasses and set them on the desk. "Mr Blackstone didn't cause you any trouble, did he?"

"No trouble, other than pausing beneath the mistletoe for a kiss," I said.

She shook her head. "He's a scoundrel, but not a bad man."

"I did want to check his movements yesterday. He said he was here."

Miss Wright nodded. "He was. The factory is open every day, including the weekends. He was stuck in his chair with his paperwork and his whisky."

"He didn't leave at any point?"

She snapped shut the diary she'd been consulting. "No. Why do you want to know about Mr Blackstone's schedule?"

We explained the situation, and her shoulders tightened. "Don't come here looking for problems. Mr Blackstone is a decent man. He'd never harm anyone. I may not have spoken kindly about him when we met, but I wouldn't want to work anywhere else."

"Even with the smell?" Ruby asked.

"Even with that!"

There were several seconds of uncomfortable silence, which I needed to diffuse with swift efficiency, or the next task would fail. "From our conversation with Mr Blackstone, I consider him a sensible sort. We're just doing our due diligence, and meant no offence."

"He's sensible enough not to get himself muddled in a murder," Miss Wright said. "And he knows we all take a little produce now and again. Nothing that would be missed, mind you. John's mistake was being greedy. That and his bad manners."

I gave the photograph of the deerhound a pointed look. "The meat is for your dog? A deerhound, isn't it?"

Her eyes lit up with pride as she turned to the photograph. "Yes, this is Fergus. He's been with me for years, ever since he was a pup. Best companion I've ever had."

Ruby, picking up on my cue, smiled warmly. "He's a beautiful dog. You must be fond of him."

"Oh, I am." Miss Wright's voice softened as she gazed at the photograph. "There's nothing like coming home to him after a long day here. He's a gentle giant, really. He loves his walks. And his treats. Mr Blackstone sometimes gives me a meat parcel for him."

I leaned against the desk. "Do you know the dogs' home in Battersea? I volunteer there."

"I do! It's an excellent place."

That was encouraging news. "The dogs' home struggles during the winter months. There are daily new arrivals. Hungry new arrivals."

Miss Wright raised an eyebrow. "It must be hard for shelters, especially with all the animals needing care. There were so many abandoned during the war."

"Exactly! Which is why we were wondering if you might help us."

"You're looking for a donation of meat?"

"Off-cuts from the factory. Produce that can't be sold and would only go to waste. The dogs would be so grateful for the extra food, just like your Fergus is."

Miss Wright hesitated for only a second before breaking into a broad smile. "That's a splendid idea, Miss Vale. And Fergus would approve, I'm sure." She stood, smoothing down her skirt. "Let's see what we can find."

"Mr Blackstone said Kevin may be able to help us." It was a tiny lie, but it gave us the perfect opportunity to question him.

"I'm sure he will. He's a strong lad and always keen to lend a hand."

"Do you need to consult with Mr Blackstone about how much we can take?" Ruby asked.

Miss Wright chuckled. "What I say goes. This way."

Within minutes, Miss Wright had found Kevin and explained the plan. He seemed happy to assist, especially when he heard the meat was going to an animal shelter.

We made our way to the loading bay, where Kevin swiftly stacked boxes of meat off-cuts. Ruby stood by her car, watching with horror as he loaded several boxes into the boot, ably instructed by Miss Wright.

"I'll never get the smell out of the upholstery," Ruby muttered.

I bit back a smile. "It's for the very best of causes."

"Yes, well." Ruby sniffed. "It's a shame the smell has to be so pernicious."

Kevin heaved another box into the car with ease. "That's the last of it."

I focused on our smiling helper. "Mr Blackstone mentioned you knew John Robinson."

"In a manner of speaking." Kevin stepped back and wiped his hands on a cloth tucked into the waistband of his trousers. "What's he gone and done this time?"

"I'm sorry to say he's dead."

There was a stunned silence.

Kevin finally huffed out a snort. "What happened?"

"We believe he was attacked."

"I'm sorry to hear that, but I can't say I'm surprised."

"It's not the first time we've heard such a comment. Did you know John well?" I asked. "We've been told he was a troublemaker."

Kevin glanced at Miss Wright, who nodded for him to answer. "I worked with him before he got himself sacked."

"What did you think of him?" I asked.

"John was a joker, but he also had a temper on him, that one. Always looking for a fight, always complaining about something or other."

"Mr Blackstone said you were friends."

"No, but he liked to talk and smoke, so we'd often be on the same breaks together. I pretended to listen while he shared his cigarettes and moaned."

"What did he complain about?"

"Everything and nothing. You know the type."

"Did John ever cause real trouble because of his temper?" I asked.

Kevin looked up, his eyes meeting mine. "He was always skirting the line, if you know what I mean. He never got caught doing anything until that last time. But he was the sort who'd steal from his own mother if he thought he could get away with it."

"Do you think he made any enemies here? Someone who might have wanted to settle a score?" I asked.

Kevin considered this for a second, then shook his head. "He was a nuisance, but no one hated him enough to kill him. Not here, anyway. Most of the lads kept their distance and didn't want to get dragged into his mess."

"Did anyone ever visit him when he was working?"

"No. At least, not that I remember." Kevin clutched the cloth. "I should get back. I don't want to get in trouble."

"Thank you, Kevin, you've been helpful," I said.

Miss Wright shooed him away, and Kevin was happy to scuttle off and get some distance from our questions. "I hope you've got everything you need."

"We have. We'll get this meat to the dogs' home right away. They'll be so happy," I said. "We're holding a Christmas party for them soon. Now, they'll have gifts and food to enjoy."

"I'm glad I could help. If you'll excuse me, I've got to ensure the last of the deliveries go out on time and Mr Blackstone hasn't fallen asleep again."

We said our goodbyes, and Ruby and I climbed into the car. The mystery of John's murder was still unsolved, but at least we knew where not to look.

# Chapter 9

After dropping off the meat at the dogs' home, it was a swift dash back to the Swan Tavern. Or at least as swift as the snow and traffic would permit.

"You must hurry! Father Bumble is expecting us for afternoon tea in five minutes. The chef has made fresh scones with cranberry and port jam. It sounds divine. There'll be cream, too." Ruby stood in the doorway of the shed, bouncing from foot to foot, while I tended to our wounded swan.

"I was happy to come out here on my own. Although I appreciate you keeping Benji and Tiberius out of the way." Benji, in particular, was always keen to assist with the animals I collected on my travels around London. Some of them appreciated his sniffing intervention less than others, and I had a feeling this hissing swan would consider Benji's inquisitive nose an indignity too far.

"I'm happy to be out here, although it's so cold." Ruby blew into her gloved hands. "I wanted to check on the swan's recovery, too. I'm so glad she survived the night."

"She's recovering well. Although I'd like to see her eat more. The wing isn't broken, which is excellent news, but she could have bruising and maybe damaged muscles. And there's a ring on one leg, suggesting she belongs to someone." I crouched in front of the magnificent bird, careful to move slowly to ensure I didn't startle her.

She was no longer hissing, but I was prepared for an attack. Swans were powerful birds and had been known to break a man's arm if he was foolish enough not to recognise the warning signs. Hissing, spread wings, lowered head, stalking. When a swan did that, you moved fast or faced the consequences.

"When will she be ready to release back into the wild?" Ruby gently held Benji back from offering a helping paw.

"It should be another day or so. Providing she stays alert, she'll be back to normal in no time," I said.

"I'm still stunned as to how the unfortunate creature came to be squashed under John's body. Do you think she got caught up in the attack?" Ruby asked.

"I can only assume so. It must have been a case of the wrong place at the wrong time. Or she was already injured and was hiding when the fight broke out. The swan wasn't fast enough to get out of the way." I gently eased my gloves on and backed away, keeping focused on the bird.

Ruby made a noise of exasperation. "Wash up before we eat. You're covered in straw! And I think there's a smear of swan droppings on your hem."

I swiped the swan's bedding from my coat. It wouldn't be the first time I looked less than pristine when protecting the abandoned angels who found themselves homeless or injured through no fault of their own.

I stepped outside and secured the door before inhaling deeply, the crisp air refreshing after the stuffy straw-filled enclosure. There was a thick layer of fresh snow on the ground, and more coming down, so we dashed inside the inn with the dogs.

Ruby waited in the sitting room with Benji and Tiberius while I freshened up. By the time I'd got down the stairs, I could hear muffled voices. I entered the sitting room, a smile on my face, and greeted Father Bumble.

"How are you both holding up?" he asked, gesturing at a chair close to the fire for me to take.

Ruby was already seated, and nodded her thanks as Baxter set down a tray of tea, festive scones, and cranberry and port jam, and then discreetly left the sitting room.

"We're made of stern stuff, but it's never a treat to find a dead body," she said.

"I'm here to offer counsel if you need a nonjudgemental ear," Father Bumble said. "And anything we discuss will be shared only with me and God. You must have a storm of emotions inside you after such an awful discovery."

"That's kind of you to offer, but we're almost used to seeing dead bodies." I settled into the comfortable chair close to the crackling fire, and Benji and Tiberius sat by my feet, their gaze on the scones.

Father Bumble startled, almost knocking over his tea cup. "You ... you are?"

"Sorry Father, Veronica didn't mean to alarm you," Ruby said. "We sometimes help the police with their enquiries, and Veronica is about to open her own private investigation agency. She's planning to have an office in Kent."

"Goodness! Whatever next? You have training in such matters?" he asked.

"Self-taught. But I've always had a knack for these things," I said. "But thank you for offering a supportive shoulder."

"It's my duty." A tremulous smile crossed Father Bumble's face. "You should hear the things that come out of people's mouths during confession. Not that I'd ever share. Even so, some of those words follow me into my sleep. Even give me the occasional nightmare."

"I can only imagine," I said. "The role of parish priest isn't just sermons on a Sunday and collections for the less fortunate."

"Indeed. Since the Great War, people's troubles have become more complicated. Many families are missing loved ones, and those who did return aren't quite themselves."

"My brother is one of them," I said.

"He should seek comfort in the Lord," Father Bumble said.

"Matthew has had trouble with his faith ever since he returned," I said. "He once asked me how such a thing could be allowed to happen? I'm afraid I had no good answer for him."

"That is sad," Father Bumble said. "We are all sent tests and trials. How we stand up to them is a measure of a man."

I bristled. "Unless that man has been through hell and back and left to fend for himself after loyally serving his country."

"Devon was saying the same thing," Ruby interrupted, knowing how sensitive I was when anyone said anything thoughtless or unkind about Matthew. "He's busy helping the young men who returned home through his psychiatry."

Father Bumble took a sip from his cup. "Of course. We all saw terrible things while we served."

"Where were you based?" I drew back my anger and focused on the scones.

"I was a noncombatant and initially stationed in Belgium. Although I moved around, going to where the need was greatest. I comforted the dying, administered last rites, and assisted soldiers with letters to family." His eyes glazed and his gaze shifted to the window before he sighed. "But now we have peace, and people can go about their lives free from fear."

"Not John," Ruby said bluntly.

Father Bumble's hand shook as he set down his cup. "Yes, that was most unfortunate. And such a terrible thing to happen to our small party."

"We heard he wasn't popular in Little Kennington," Ruby said. "Will there be many people mourning his passing?"

"We all deserve to be mourned," Father Bumble said. "And I seek goodness in everyone, even those who don't attend church. He is in my prayers."

"We all worship in our own ways," I said softly.

"Of course. But even if my sermons weren't to his taste, attending church is an excellent way to meet your neighbours," Father Bumble said. "I suggested such a thing to him several times, but he didn't take me seriously."

I suppressed a smile. I was familiar with the priests and vicars in many London churches, often visiting to learn pertinent details for my obituary notices. Churches were excellent places for gossip, with the ladies, in particular, sharing secrets over a cup of strong tea and a biscuit after the service. I was convinced some of them attended more for the gossip than for God.

"I do hope the police arrive soon," Father Bumble said. "That poor man needs to be laid to rest."

"Eddie is determined to reach them. He's convinced the telephone will be working soon," I said. "Although if he doesn't get a dial tone soon, I fear he'll insist on walking to the station."

"Not with his leg! He'll make himself sick over Christmas."

"Mitzie won't allow him to do anything foolish. But if the police are unavailable, we should act. John is in a storage shed next to the injured swan. It's not fitting accommodation for either of them."

Father Bumble took a scone. "Ah. Yes. The swan. How is the creature?"

"I've just been to check on her. She's recovering well."

"No thanks to John squashing the poor dear," Ruby said. "It's strange how they came to be in the alley at the same time."

"Life is full of strange and wonderful things. And sadly, accidents do happen." Father Bumble dropped crumbs onto his lap as he ate his scone.

"What if John's death wasn't an accident?" I asked.

He blinked owlishly behind his glasses. "You mentioned that on the afternoon we found him. I assumed John slipped on ice and hit his head."

"It's possible, although I was first on the scene with Benji and Tiberius and saw that John had red marks on his face and wrists," I said.

"From the fall?"

"It's hard to say."

"I wouldn't concern yourself with such details. I've taken plenty of tumbles in the snow, ice, or even in the damp. Sometimes, for no obvious reason at all." Father Bumble heaped jam onto what was left of his scone. "I'm convinced I have two left feet. I always have bruises in the most extraordinary places. But when a parishioner is in need, I endeavour to get to them, no matter the conditions."

"Since you're so hardy, have you volunteered to walk to the police station?" Ruby asked with a butter wouldn't melt tilt to her head.

Father Bumble's cheeks flushed. "If I was called into service, I would act. But I must confess, my bunions are playing up, so I'm not certain I could hobble that far. The walk to the park so we could skate was a chore I endured so as not to upset dear Mitzie."

Father Bumble seemed happy to talk while he munched on the scones, so I opened up, bringing him into my confidence. "I've been wondering about the argument I witnessed between Devon and John. Did you notice them having words when we were skating?"

"Not especially. I was too busy trying not to fall and break anything. When Colonel Draper spoke to Devon, he said it was something to do with a young lady."

"Perhaps you know her," Ruby said. "She most likely lives in Little Kennington."

Father Bumble furrowed his brow and took another sip of tea. "John was a charmer, and he enjoyed the company of ladies, but I don't believe they shared an interest in the same lady. Devon has recently become engaged."

I leaned forward in my seat. "Perhaps that was the woman John was interested in, too."

"I think that unlikely. Elizabeth, Devon's fiancée, doesn't live in Little Kennington." Father Bumble pressed his hands into a prayer position and rested his chin on the top of his fingers. "I suppose Elizabeth could have met John when she visited Devon, but I'd be surprised if their paths had ever crossed."

"Could John have said something inappropriate about Elizabeth and made Devon angry?" I said.

"Why would he do such a thing? There would be no point. Devon and Elizabeth are childhood sweethearts. They plan on marrying in the village church." A dreamy smile crossed Father Bumble's face. "It's such a pretty setting, and there's a small village green where couples have their photographs taken after the service, if the weather allows."

"It sounds charming," Ruby said. "Have they set a date for the wedding?"

Father Bumble nodded. "September of next year. And I'll be proud to marry them."

I exchanged a glance with Ruby. Why would Devon claim he was arguing with John over a woman if he was happily engaged to Elizabeth? Had Devon lied? He'd mentioned she was a close friend, so perhaps there wasn't a romantic connection. And from what I'd overheard of the conversation, Devon had been warning

John to stop doing something. Had he meant to stop toying with a lady's affections?

"It's a pity you didn't stay on the ice all morning," Ruby said. "You could have information to help us figure out this puzzle."

"It's good of you to think I might be useful, but I don't see this sad situation as a puzzle. I'm certain John's death was an accident," Father Bumble replied.

"Where did you go when you left the ice?" I asked. "I don't think I saw you for over an hour. And you seemed to be having such fun."

"Goodness! You are observant." Father Bumble pinched his chin between his thumb and finger. "I suppose I must have been gone that long. I admitted defeat when my bunions started throbbing. I'd also spilled hot cocoa all over myself. I didn't realise what I'd done until an impertinent young lady laughed at me, so I came back here, changed my clothes, and rested my feet."

"Did you see anyone when you were here?" Perhaps Father Bumble had seen Devon at the inn, too. It would be handy if they could alibi for each other.

Father Bumble brushed a hand down his front. "I let Baxter know my plan, and he was kind enough to return with me and arrange for coffee. We sat and had a cup together. He's an excellent fellow, and so loyal to the household."

"Isn't he a darling? I wish I had a Baxter of my own," Ruby said. "My life would run like clockwork, and I'd never be late for anything."

"That would indeed be a miracle," I murmured.

"We discussed the Christmas luncheon, which I'm most looking forward to," Father Bumble said, a hint of excitement in his voice.

"Baxter always makes sure people are well fed," I said.

"The Drapers are benevolent and generous hosts." Father Bumble patted his round belly. "And they're happy to open their doors to people and make sure they feel welcome when they move to the village. Even John."

"Did John have any family?" I asked.

"No. I suggested he returned home for Christmas, but he said everyone had passed. It's such a shame, but that's what war does to a family." Father Bumble bowed his head for a few seconds. "But I've spoken to Mrs Draper and assured her no one would think less of her if we continue the celebrations. We must give thanks for the birth of our Lord."

"I expect he enjoyed a party, too." Ruby said. "There was that big event with the water and wine, wasn't there?"

Father Bumble's benign expression tightened a fraction. "I expect you'll both attend Midnight Mass. I'll be assisting with the service alongside Father Connell."

"We wouldn't miss it," I said swiftly.

We spent the next few minutes in pleasant conversation, discussing our Christmas plans and eating scones. Since Father Bumble had an alibi and no motive, we could scrub him off the suspect list. Although I had hoped he'd provide useful clues to reveal Devon's possible involvement.

Once we'd drunk our tea, we made our excuses and left Father Bumble finishing off the scones, which he did with remarkable vigour.

"One suspect down," Ruby whispered as we left the sitting room.

"Father Bumble wasn't really a suspect. But he also wasn't much help, since he's too discreet to reveal his congregations' dark secrets," I replied.

"More's the pity. I adore a scandal. Who's next?"

I grimaced. "We need to tackle our dear friend Colonel Edward Draper."

"Surely not. Eddie can't be a suspect!"

"No, I don't believe he'd do such a thing as murder a man at his wife's Christmas party, but we must be thorough," I said. "And we need to convince him we're a help, not a hindrance in this investigation."

"Eddie will have to accept our help if there's to be no police involvement," Ruby said. "He knows how useful we are in a crisis."

"As accepting as he was of that during the war, he's pricklier in peace time." I pulled back my shoulders. "But we've dealt with equally fearsome foe and survived."

Ruby grabbed a sprig of holly from the mantle we passed and brandished it in front of her. "It's time to break in the old war horse!"

# Chapter 10

It only took a moment to locate Eddie in the billiard room. He was alone.

"He won't like to be disturbed while he's in there," Ruby whispered as we lingered outside the door with the dogs, peeking through a small crack.

"He'd expect nothing less from us," I said. "He doesn't enjoy wishy-washy behaviour. Or cowardice."

"How shall we handle him?" Ruby asked.

"Directly. And with no hidden agendas. Let me deal with him. If you don't want to be here, Benji and Tiberius would appreciate a walk, even though the conditions are terrible. I don't think they've forgiven us for not taking them to the meat factory."

Ruby chuckled. "Although I'd rather face a firing squad than Eddie in a bad mood, I'm sticking with you."

I tapped on the slightly open door. "Colonel, may we have a word?"

"Is that you, Vale?"

I eased the door open. "It won't take long."

He waved us in. "Don't stand on ceremony. What's troubling you?"

I settled into a comfortable plaid chair with padded arms, the dogs next to me. "We still have concerns about John's death."

"I thought as much." His nostrils flared.

I pressed on before I lost my nerve. "As you're aware, we're not sure his death was an accident. Have you any thoughts on the matter?"

Eddie's eyebrows rose slowly, but he didn't dismiss my question. "It must have been an accident. It's the logical explanation. We both saw his body."

I drew in a steadying breath. "We've always spoken frankly to each other, so don't dismiss my worry. You keep saying it was an accident, but there's something else going on. We're hearing things about John's character that don't add up. He wasn't popular in Little Kennington."

Eddie took a long moment to consider my words before sighing. "I wondered on more than one occasion if John would meet a sticky end."

"What makes you say that?" Ruby had taken the seat next to me.

"Because I can't abide liars. And I know few people who do."

I settled my hands in my lap. Finally, we were getting somewhere. "What did he lie to you about?"

Eddie shook his head as if attempting to dismiss his doubts. "We shouldn't talk about this. Murder will ruin everything for Mitzie. She has her heart set on a perfect Christmas gathering. This is her favourite time of year. We should settle this as an accident. It's not as if John will be missed."

My frustration softened. Eddie would do anything to make Mitzie content. "If this wasn't an accident, we must seek the truth. What did John lie to you about?"

Eddie grumbled his annoyance at being forced to reconsider his stance and potentially upset his dear wife. "Not so much to me. He never had the nerve to attempt any of his dubious nonsense with me, but I heard village rumours. Over exaggerated claims of his time in the war. My understanding is men embellish their bravado because the ladies like it."

"You've always valued honesty," I said. "Did you have words with John about his lies?"

"A few words were said. That was all that was needed. I got my message across."

"You didn't like John?" Ruby asked.

"I never hid my dislike of the man. And if it were up to me, he wouldn't have joined our party, but I can never refuse Mitzie anything. She convinced me John was lonely and trying to impress his new neighbours by making up stories, and that he meant no harm by it." Eddie harrumphed. "Tell that to the real war heroes who never made it home."

"Mitzie simply wants everyone to enjoy the festivities," I said.

"There's nothing worse than being alone at Christmas," Ruby said.

"It wouldn't be so bad with the right food, the wireless on, and a decent bottle of wine to keep you company." Eddie gave her a level look. "Still, I see how some may find it trying. Christmas is a time for family and good friends."

I glanced at Ruby. Now, for the most difficult part of this conversation. "I noticed Mitzie couldn't tempt you to put on your skates when we were at the park."

Eddie patted his leg. "My old injury advises caution when doing anything as foolish as putting my feet onto two blades and sliding across ice. Mitzie wouldn't want me laid up over Christmas."

"Does it trouble you terribly?" Ruby asked.

"The cold weather doesn't help," Eddie said. "I suggested we spend the winter abroad, but Mitzie would have none of it. She wanted to be surrounded by friends and family, and who was I to argue? I expect she's wishing we'd gone away now, so we weren't embroiled in this situation."

"A situation you now agree could be murder?" I asked.

His gaze went to the frozen vista outside the tavern. "Mitzie scolds me for being stubborn-headed."

"I do the same to Veronica," Ruby said brightly. "You are so similar. It's why you get along famously."

I shared a smile with Eddie.

"You've cracked open the possibility of murder to me," he finally said. "There's even been a time or two when I've been tempted to wring the blighter's neck."

"Then it's a good job John was whacked over the head and not strangled!" I said.

Eddie grunted a reply.

"Where did you go when you grew bored by watching the skating?" I asked as calmly as I dared. "I lost sight of you for a while."

Eddie paused for a heartbeat. "Did you now?"

"Perhaps you found a roaring fire in a local pub." Although I considered Eddie a dear friend, he had been missing for a portion of that day, and I had to make sure he had nothing to do with what happened to John.

His shrewd expression suggested he knew what I was prodding at, but he nodded. "I noticed the local tobacconist had my favourite brand in the window, so we took a walk and visited the shop. I know the chap who runs the place. He's an excellent fellow, so I thought we'd stop by and exchange pleasantries."

"Who were you with?"

"Mitzie, of course. I convinced her to come off the ice before she broke a bone."

His alibi would be easy to check with Mitzie and the shop owner, and I recalled Eddie and Mitzie returning just as we broke for warm drinks and cake. I didn't enjoy having our friends on the suspect list for a murder. But it tallied so far. Mitzie had disappeared around the same time as Eddie, and I couldn't begin to believe they'd worked together to commit such a dreadful crime.

"That hound of yours certainly has a nose on him," Eddie said. "He sniffed out the problem before anyone else and raced off to see what he could do about it."

"I wouldn't have it any other way," I said. "Benji has helped me out of numerous scrapes."

"He wouldn't need to if you kept out of trouble and got yourself a sensible job." Eddie's smile held a hint of knowing slyness. "But of course, you'd find life terribly dull if you weren't involving yourself in other people's business."

"It's not something I seek out," I said. "But I won't apologise for having a curious nature, or for wanting to help the less fortunate."

"I could tell you what that curiosity will bring you, but you won't listen to sense." Eddie smoothed his moustache with his fingers.

I wouldn't be deterred by his stern tone. "Were John and Mitzie close?"

"She always takes an interest in the single men that move to the village. She's forever on the hunt to get them paired up. Mitzie told me she wants everyone to be as blissfully happy as she is."

"Doesn't that bother you?"

Eddie lifted his glass and took a drink. "Why should it?"

"She's an attractive woman."

"An attractive married woman," Eddie said. "And loyal to me."

"Of course. But that doesn't always stop men from showing an inappropriate interest," I said.

Eddie snorted. "They can show all the interest they like, but her head's not for turning."

I'd been around Mitzie and Eddie enough times to know they had a happy marriage, but I was also aware Eddie had a rotten temper and a jealous streak.

"You never noticed John flirting with Mitzie?" I asked.

The question earned me another snort. "The man would have been a fool to try."

"So, he didn't?" I pressed.

Eddie set down his glass and fixed me with a steely glare. "If he was imprudent enough to waste his time flirting with my wife, he'd have felt the sharp side of her tongue. Mitzie is a sweet girl, but she has high moral standards. If John made inappropriate advances, she'd have set him straight."

"Did she ever tell you John was inappropriate with her?" Ruby asked. "When we met at the tavern on our first evening, he was quick to be overly friendly with me. Veronica had to put John in his place on more than one occasion."

"Hah! I've no doubt she did." Eddie chuckled to himself. "But no, if he had, I'd have known about it. John may have pushed the envelope in some areas of his life, but he'd have been a buffoon to risk isolating himself by overstepping the mark with Mitzie. She has an excellent reputation and a high standing in our village community. She'd have only needed to say the word, and John would have been in trouble. It's easy to find yourself blackballed in a small place like Little Kennington if you don't follow the rules."

"He's in trouble now," I said.

"Quite. The situation is unfortunate, but it's a matter for the police, should they ever get here."

I drew in a breath to argue with him, but he raised a hand.

"Enough talk of John. Everything is under control. But I do need your help on a matter dear to Mitzie's heart."

"What would that be?" I asked.

"She's distraught that our celebrations will be viewed as inappropriate. She spent time with Father Bumble, talking about what we should do. He's a simple chap, but his heart is in the right place, and after a quick word from me, he convinced her things should go ahead as planned. No one will mind, will they? We can hardly cancel Christmas!"

"Of course not. How would you like us to help?"

"Tell Mitzie how much you're looking forward to the Christmas luncheon and gift giving. She's worried she'll appear crass, being so happy when someone has died. Even if that death means people will sleep more easily in their beds."

"That'll be simple, since we're very much looking forward to the day," Ruby said. "Consider it done."

"You mentioned the police. Have you spoken to them?" I asked.

Eddie sighed. "You won't leave this matter alone, will you?"

"I will. Once it's resolved to my satisfaction."

"You're a stubborn girl."

I tilted my head and waited, perfectly prepared to show him how stubborn I could be.

Eddie growled out another sigh. "Yes. I've been in touch with them."

"Why didn't you say anything to us?" I stood from my seat.

"Because, Vale, you don't need to know all of my movements."

I huffed out my disagreement, which only made him chortle.

"Settle yourself. I planned on gathering everyone and providing an update. I needed to wait until you were all here, so I wouldn't have to repeat the same story half a dozen times."

"What news do you have?" I glanced at the door. If the telephone line was operational, I could contact Jacob.

Eddie shook his head at my persistence, but relented. "There was a train derailment not far from here. The police have been tied up with that. Dreadful mess, apparently. They're sending someone to speak to our party as soon as they can."

"What did you tell them about John's death?" Ruby asked.

"That there were no obvious signs of foul play. I explained the situation, and they seemed content with my conclusion that it was an accident." Eddie lifted a hand once more. "And before you mention the marks on his body, they can be accounted for."

"But you said you were open to the possibility that it could have been murder," I said.

A stubborn glint appeared in his eyes. "Why look for trouble when there's nothing to be gained from it?"

"There's plenty to be gained," I said. "We could have a killer among us."

"What tosh and nonsense. We know everyone in the party. Why waste your time and spoil the gathering?"

I lifted my chin. "To ensure justice is done. It's the right thing to do."

"You and your justice crusades."

"Someone has to crusade," I said.

Eddie exhaled loudly through his nose. "You're like those troublesome suffragettes. At least you've got the brains for it, I suppose."

"Does that mean you won't stop us from asking more questions?"

"As if I have a choice in the matter," Eddie said. "I could yell at you in a tone that made a squadron of seasoned soldiers cringe, and you wouldn't bat an eyelid."

I smiled demurely.

"I ask one thing of you, though. Don't spoil the festive season. Mitzie will be heartbroken if you abandon her to poke at the dead. You do that enough with your day job."

"We can party and investigate," Ruby said. "When people are more relaxed, they let their guard down, so we could learn something useful."

"Or end up neck-deep in trouble and getting on the wrong side of the police," Eddie said.

"The police will see we're only being helpful." I sometimes wished Jacob still worked locally. It made life so much easier when I was investigating trouble.

"I should find Mitzie." Eddie stood. "She was talking about venturing out into the snow to buy more gifts. She wants people to have a party to remember for the right reasons, not because a guest didn't make it to Christmas Day."

"Tell her not to bother with more extravagance. We have everything we need right here," I said.

"My girl loves to overcompensate. And my wallet takes a punishing hit every time she does." He nodded at us, patted Benji and Tiberius as he passed them, and left the room.

"What do you think?" Ruby said once the door was closed and we were alone. "Eddie only entertained the possibility of foul play for a moment, and he didn't hide his dislike of John."

"He never hides his dislike of anyone who gets on his wrong side," I said. "But did he downplay the issue of John flirting with Mitzie? Eddie has a temper. We've both seen it."

"He also has an alibi," Ruby said. "He was with Mitzie, so he couldn't have been anywhere near John when he was killed."

We sat in the silent room as we mulled over what we'd discovered so far. Eddie had an alibi, as did Mitzie, since they were together at the tobacconists. Father Bumble and Baxter alibied for each other by having tea at the tavern. That left only Devon in our party as a suspect. Perhaps our initial misgivings had been correct.

"John was arguing with a man named Nathan in the public bar the night before he died," I said.

"Yes! Baxter said his name was Nathan Burrows."

"It was a heated row."

"Nathan could have waited for a chance to get his revenge. Or perhaps he arranged to meet John at the tavern the next day. Things got intense, and blows were exchanged."

"We need to speak to Aggie and find out more about the mysterious Nathan. If he's local, we should visit him. She knows to inform me if he makes an appearance, but it would do no harm to remind her."

The door burst open, and Mitzie appeared, looking breathless. "There you are. Hurry! The police are finally here!"

# Chapter 11

We dashed after Mitzie, but I slowed as we approached the two police officers standing just inside the main entrance to the tavern, and a flash of disappointment hit me. Of course, I'd expected to see Jacob. It was an old habit. My former nemesis and now business partner and dear friend, sometimes more than a friend, was on his own journey. A journey I was in the middle of, and happy to be so.

I didn't recognise either officer who stood in their thick coats and winter mufflers, a light dusting of snow on their shoulders and hats.

Eddie was with them, deep in conversation. He turned when we approached. "Not now, Vale. I have everything in hand."

"You're here about Mr Robinson. I'm happy to let you know my findings so far." It wasn't the best of manners to ignore Eddie, but I had to know what was going on from the police, and not have it distilled by Eddie's stern, practical filter.

Eddie scowled at me, but then sighed, knowing I was going nowhere until I got the information I desired.

"This is Inspector Harold Finchley and his colleague, Sergeant Benjamin Brown."

I nodded in greeting and introduced myself and Ruby. "Inspector Finchley, do you now lead on murder investigations in this part of London? I'm a little out of the loop regarding who replaced Jacob Templeton."

He made several spluttering sounds. "Murder! I'm not sure where that idea came from."

"From the evidence, sir," I said.

Inspector Finchley's small, dark eyes widened. "Did you say you're Veronica Vale?"

"I am. I don't believe we've met before, but I'm assuming you're an experienced officer if they sent you to deal with this situation."

He huffed out an indignant breath. "We may not have met in person, but I feel like we have. Your reputation precedes you. Former Inspector Jacob Templeton had many colourful words when describing your involvement in police matters that had nothing to do with you."

Sergeant Brown's chuckle died when I speared him with a cold glare. "That is all in the past. We are now the firmest of friends. Business partners, in fact."

Inspector Finchley didn't look convinced. I'd have to work hard to gain his trust. Perhaps getting Jacob to have a word may help. Having a stranger involved in this matter was less than ideal, especially since it appeared Inspector Finchley was already resisting the idea of murder before even undertaking an investigation.

I pushed on. "Have you examined John's body? That should answer the question as to why I believe this wasn't an accidental death."

Inspector Finchley looked startled. "Not yet. And with the train derailment at Liverpool Street Station, we haven't had an experienced person to spare."

"Yes. That is a terrible tragedy—"

"Thirteen dead!"

I bowed my head for a second. "But John was murdered."

"Let's not discuss this now," Eddie said. "The police will soon have everything under control. We have nothing to concern ourselves with."

"You should interview all of us," I said to Inspector Finchley. "We all associated with John just before he died, so you must find out if he had any enemies."

He exchanged an astonished glance with his sergeant. "I'll ensure everyone is spoken to, but only to confirm what we already know about Mr Robinson."

"You were acquainted with him? He's not lived in Little Kennington for long."

Inspector Finchley hesitated and looked at Eddie.

He grunted. "Veronica will only probe and prod until she gets an answer, so you may as well make this as painless as possible for yourself."

"Mr Robinson was known to us," Inspector Finchley said after another short pause. "And not for the right reasons."

"He had a criminal record?" I asked.

"I'm unable to go into that level of details with a civilian."

"What can you tell us?" Eddie asked.

"Let me just say we weren't surprised to learn he'd been found dead in an alley after a fall. The man often drank to excess, and when he did, he was a public nuisance."

"Perhaps he had a few too many drinks at the party," I said, "but John was still standing at the end of the night. And although he was a little worse for wear the following morning, I didn't see him drinking again. He was killed during the day, so an excess of alcohol wasn't the cause of death. The man was murdered."

"You must stop saying it was murder." Inspector Finchley's tone was sharp. "We will inspect his body, but we aren't looking at this incident as suspicious. Not after everything Colonel Draper has told us."

My fists clenched. This fellow had clearly received his education at the College for Nitwits and Stubborn Nincompoops.

"Mitzie, why not take Veronica and Ruby to the library?" Eddie suggested. "I'll finish up with the police and then join you."

I opened my mouth to protest, but a sharp pinch from Ruby on the underside of my arm had me clamping my mouth shut. Nothing I said would make a difference. Inspector Finchley had made his decision about John's demise, and he wasn't for turning. It was frustrating, but I wouldn't be defeated in getting to the truth.

After some gentle cajoling from Mitzie and Ruby, I walked away, scowling at the prospect a killer may get away with a terrible crime due to all this pointless dithering.

Once we were inside the library, the door closed, Mitzie clasped my hands and stood firm in front of me. "Don't be angry. I'm sure the police know what they're doing."

"Clearly, they don't! And the brief interviews they'll conduct will be for show," I said. "I'll be surprised if they even check motives or alibis."

Mitzie's pretty blue eyes widened. "Eddie has spoken to me about your concerns, but what reason would anyone have for killing John?"

I returned her fierce grip. "Why did you invite John to spend Christmas here?"

"I've already said that he seemed like the fun, partying sort. I thought he'd be entertaining to have around."

"Did John ever behave inappropriately with you?"

Her head jerked back a fraction. "Never!"

Ruby touched Mitzie's arm. "You don't have to hide anything from us. We won't judge. John was free with his hands when we spent the evening together, and you're an attractive woman. A man would have to be blind not to appreciate your charms."

Mitzie let go of one of my hands and lightly patted her neatly coiffed hair. "I'm not sure what you're implying."

"Perhaps John overstepped the boundaries," I said as gently as possible.

Mitzie went quiet for an uncomfortable length of time, but I was determined to remain silent until she spoke. Eventually, she sighed. "I said nothing because I didn't want Eddie to learn about John's behaviour."

"What did John do?" Ruby asked.

"Nothing, but it was boldly implied what he'd like to do with me, and he was keen for us to be alone so it could happen." Her cheeks flushed. "I was mortified. I didn't know what to say to him."

"The rotter!" Ruby said. "No wonder someone did him in."

"Please continue, Mitzie. What happened?" I asked.

"We'd met several times since John's move to Little Kennington. I thought he was charming, but a touch insincere with his compliments. Then I heard him making exaggerated claims about his service in the Great War. I know about the struggles our men went through, and although Eddie rarely talks about it, it left physical and emotional scars he'll live with for the rest of his life."

"It must have been difficult to hear John bragging," I said.

"I thought it best to keep quiet. After all, we must get on with our neighbours, especially in a village as small as Little Kennington. But when one of the younger, more impressionable girls in the village said she wanted to marry John because he was a war hero and would look after her, I had to step in," Mitzie said.

"Did you tell her not to waste her time?" Ruby asked.

"I gently nudged her towards a more suitable man, then I approached John. I had a bridge evening planned with friends, but I left early so I could stop at the pub. John could be found there most evenings."

"And you confronted him?" I asked.

"I did it in the most Mitzie-like way I could. I told him some of the ladies were under a false impression of him, and it wouldn't be right if they continued to believe everything they'd heard. I pretended somebody else was making up his heroic war stories and they weren't coming from him."

"How did John react?"

"He was angry at first, but then he realised he could get away with his lies. He promised me none of the information had come from him, and he'd set everyone straight."

"Did you believe him?" Ruby said.

"I ... I wasn't sure, but I like to give everybody the benefit of the doubt. We chatted for a few moments, and I was about to leave when he suggested I stay. He wanted to get to know me better and was sure he could show me a better time than my, as he put it, 'stuffy old husband' could."

"I hope you gave him a sharp slap," Ruby said.

"I was embarrassed and grateful no one else overheard. Times have changed, but it's easy to get a black mark on one's reputation. When John realised he'd offended me, he was horrified. He was full of remorse and almost in tears. He said he hadn't been himself since coming home, and he was lonely."

"That's no reason to act like a cad when you've been nothing but kind to him," Ruby said.

"John told me the woman he'd left behind had promised to wait for him, but she married another man while he was away. It left him bitter and terribly alone." Mitzie pressed her lips together. "There was also an incident after a luncheon I hosted, when I had to set him right again using my butter knife. He blamed it on the drink that time."

"And even after that encounter, you still took pity on him," I said on a sigh. "So much so that you invited him to spend Christmas with you?"

"John said he had nobody. There are no siblings or parents left alive. He was all alone in this world, and that's a terrible place to find yourself. I invited him to spend Christmas with us, on the understanding there would be no more propositions. We were strictly friends."

"And of course, he jumped on that," I said.

Mitzie bit her bottom lip. "Have I been naïve? Was there a snake hiding in our midst?"

"A slithering charmer," Ruby said.

"And now a dead snake. And I'm certain, after seeing John's injuries, somebody killed him," I said. "I just need to figure out who and why."

"You can't think I had anything to do with it." Mitzie's eyes were wide as she stared at me. "I know I had a reason to dislike him, but when John remembered his manners, he was fun. He always brought a dull evening to life."

"Of course, we don't think you were involved in his death," Ruby said. "You're the sweetest person among us."

"But we do need to know where you went when you left the park," I said. Mitzie was a dear friend, but I couldn't let that cloud my judgement.

Her expression grew serious. "Of course. If you think somebody hurt John, you must get to the truth."

I waited for her to continue.

"Eddie was getting grumpy watching us when we were skating. He'd passed a tobacconist he wanted to visit and told me to stay on the ice with you, but I wanted to go with him. We walked back to the shop, and while I browsed the flavoured cigarillos, Eddie made his purchases. Then we came back just in time for tea and cake."

I relaxed and the tension that had gripped my stomach unfurled. It was awful to think Eddie or Mitzie could be responsible for what happened to John, but with their matching alibis, I was convinced it wasn't them. Almost. I had to do my due diligence, and would visit the tobacconist. But as far as I was concerned, they were innocent.

"You won't tell Eddie what happened with John, will you?" Mitzie asked. "There's no point in getting him riled up over John's bad behaviour. Not now he's dead."

"We won't breathe a word of it," Ruby said.

There was a tap on the door, and Eddie opened it, his expression set to stern. "The police are checking John's body."

"I hope you told them to be thorough, and to watch out for the swan. The last thing we need is for them to get nipped and rush out before completing their inspection," I said.

Eddie exhaled a combination of a grunt and a sigh. "Vale, I don't appreciate your interference. Neither do the police. Before you blundered in, I had a handle on the situation."

"I want to know what happened to John as much as everybody else," I said. "The police are really not considering this a murder?"

"From the information they've gathered so far, it would seem not. But that is for them to determine."

"You must have suggested something when you reached them on the telephone."

"I stated the facts."

I settled my hands on my hips. "Did you not think to even mention the possibility of foul play? After everything we discussed?"

Mitzie squeaked, knowing I'd just poked a moustachioed bear.

Eddie ignored my bluntness. "They'll speak to everyone in a few moments after collecting any evidence from the body. After that, they'll close the case if they see fit. Mitzie, come with me. They'll speak with us first."

Mitzie squeezed my hand, then hurried after her husband, who gave me a warning look before closing the door behind him.

"Oh, golly. I don't like the look on your face," Ruby said to me.

"The police may be more interested in their Christmas goose than in catching a killer, but I'm not. And neither are you. We're giving the gift of finding out who killed John, even if the police won't help."

# Chapter 12

While we waited for the police to interview each of us in turn, I attempted to reach Jacob on the telephone. For a few seconds, I obtained a crackly line, but it swiftly died, and no amount of jiggling the cable or turning the dial would make it work.

I set the telephone down in its cradle with a frustrated sigh. I was eager to discover if Jacob had uncovered any information about what happened to my father. The evidence he'd collected so far was from conversations and hearsay. We needed actual proof my father hadn't taken his own life by jumping off Beachy Head, but had, in fact, been attacked. And if that was the truth, I'd hunt down the villain and ensure justice was severely meted out.

"Veronica, have you realised what time it is?" Ruby hurried along the corridor, wearing her outdoor coat and sensible boots.

"You're going out?" I inspected my watch.

"We need to pick up the donations for the dogs' home. We said we'd deliver them this afternoon for the party."

I'd been so focused on what was going on with John and my personal issues that I'd let my impeccable organisational skills lapse. "Oh, my word! We can't let them down."

"Baxter was good enough to clear the car of the fresh snow," Ruby said, "so we can be on the road in a jiffy."

For a second, I was torn between staying to ensure the police did a thorough job and not wanting to let down my beloved dogs' home. I'd been put in charge of obtaining donations of food, blankets, and old newspapers so the dogs would have a comfortable Christmas. The staff and volunteers had also arranged a small party today, where the dogs would receive a gift and be given endless amounts of cuddles.

My desire to spend time with adorable animals appropriately won out. The police would have to wait for our statements. That was if they even bothered to gather them.

"You find Benji and Tiberius," I said. "The last time I saw them, they were sneaking off to the kitchen. Then we'll be on our way. And no dallying."

Ruby gave an unladylike snort. "You were the one with your head in the clouds, thinking about murder and your gentleman friend. What are we calling Jacob these days? Your friend? Partner? Fiancé?"

"Quite. Quite. I won't make a habit of it. Chop, chop. The dogs are waiting for their gifts."

Five minutes later, we were tucked in Ruby's car, Benji and Tiberius on the back seat as Ruby navigated the busy London traffic to get us to our first destination: Baldwick and Baxter. They were a distribution company that transported a variety of produce around the country. The owner, Mr Baldwick, had adopted three dogs from the dogs' home, and was a stalwart supporter of our endeavours to get more strays off the streets and find them loving homes. Every year, he organised fundraising events and put the money towards Christmas gifts for the animals in our care. His warehouse was also the drop off point for offerings of blankets, food, and newspapers from generous benefactors.

"How do you think the police are going with the interviews?" Ruby waited behind a crowded omnibus while passengers disembarked onto the snowy path.

"I know neither of the officers, but from Inspector Finchley's stubborn behaviour, I fear he's set his mind on one outcome, so he won't dig too far."

"But we intend to?"

"Naturally. If the police refuse to see this matter for what it is, it's our civic duty to ensure the right path is followed." I gripped the car seat as the back wheels slid when Ruby pulled away.

"I don't think they're in a hurry. As I left the kitchen, a tray loaded with tea and cake was being taken up to them."

"How typical. Thinking of their stomachs before doing their job. At least that gives us more time to spend with the dogs."

Ruby glanced at me. "Veronica! You can be harsh."

"Plain speaking is never harsh."

"The poor chaps may have been dealing with the train crash. They wouldn't have had time to eat."

"There was a fresh fried egg deposit on Inspector Finchley's tie."

She chuckled. "It's a pity you couldn't get through to Jacob. He would give you the measure of the man and let you know if he's got the chops to deal with this matter."

"I've obtained Inspector Finchley's measure myself, and unfortunately, it's unappealing."

"I could attempt a gentle flirt to see if we can soften him up," Ruby said. "But I suspect he's all practical and no fun."

"I'll see how he deals with my interview," I said. "If it's as lukewarm as I anticipate, the man will be of no use to us."

"Until you met Jacob, you thought no man was useful," Ruby said.

"And most of the time, I was correct. But there are exceptions to every rule."

"Like Mr Baldwick. If he wasn't over fifty, already married, and missing most of his teeth, I'd consider him the perfect catch," Ruby said.

"He has a most generous spirit," I said.

"A man's character often makes him repugnant or twice as handsome," Ruby said. "And after my last ghastly encounter with a handsome face, I shall be sure to inspect thoroughly my next beau's character, rather than flirt and flush over a strong pair of arms and a winning smile."

"I never had the opportunity to inspect Alfonso's character," I said.

"Now I have perspective, it was sorely lacking," Ruby said. "I was such a ninny over him and overlooked his obvious flaws because I thought I could get him to change. But there was so much to change. It would have been an impossible task."

"I used to think change was impossible, too," I said. "But I believe a small shift is achievable. I've mellowed over time."

Ruby chortled. "Perhaps a fraction. And we know who we have to thank for that."

"Benji and Tiberius?"

She laughed even more. "Jacob! You're a hard nut to crack, but he was persistent."

"The man is more stubborn than me," I said.

"And that's exactly what you need. No nonsense. You need someone straight-talking and strong. Practical, too."

"I have that with Jacob." I smiled to myself. Yes, people could change, and sometimes, it was good when they did.

Ten minutes later, we arrived at the warehouse where we were picking up the supplies. The place was bustling, with last-minute Christmas orders being dispatched, men hurrying back and forth, filling vehicles as they yelled to each other.

We enquired as to where Mr Baldwick was, and he appeared a moment later dressed in a startling bright red suit.

"Season's greetings to both of you!" He pressed a kiss to our cheeks. "I have a surprise for you."

"Is it your marvellous suit?" Ruby asked. "What a glorious colour!"

He roared with laughter. "I'm playing Father Christmas. Come this way, ladies." Mr Baldwick led us through the bustling warehouse, weaving between workers, crates, and vehicles with an energy that belied his age.

The sight that awaited us made Ruby and me come to a sudden halt. In the corner of the warehouse, towering high, was a veritable mountain of boxes, all neatly labelled. Dog food, blankets, treats—more than enough to keep the dogs in comfort for weeks, if not months.

"Good gracious," Ruby muttered, blinking at the sheer scale of it. "I had no idea there'd be so much."

Mr Baldwick grinned, his eyes twinkling beneath his bushy brows. "I told you I had a surprise. We did a big drive this year. Everyone chipped in, and we've gathered more than ever. Even the staff donated."

I felt a surge of gratitude. "This is wonderful. You can be assured, the dogs will be well taken care of this Christmas."

"That's what I like to hear." He rubbed his hands together. "Shall we get cracking?"

Ruby's smile faltered. "I'm thrilled, truly, but there's not a chance this is all fitting into my car."

"Never fear, dear ladies. You didn't think I'd let you haul this on your own, did you? No, no. We'll get one of the lads to help with a van." He turned and whistled sharply, catching the attention of one of the workers, and a lean young man came trotting over.

"Pete. Get the van ready, will you? These ladies need to make a delivery to Battersea, and they've got a few too many gifts for the dogs to manage on their own."

Pete nodded. "Right away, sir."

A minute later, he pulled the van up to the loading bay before he rolled up his sleeves, and we began loading the boxes into the van and car.

Once the van was packed, our car was ready, and Benji and Tiberius had been given endless amounts of treats and pats from Mr Baldwick, we set off for Battersea, calling out our thanks and lots of Merry Christmases.

The drive was smooth, and the snow that had threatened earlier held off, leaving us with clear skies and a safe passage to our waggy-tail filled destination.

As we pulled up to the dogs' home, we were greeted with cheerful waves from the staff and volunteers, who were bustling around preparing for the party. The sight of Pete's van pulling in behind us caused a stir of excitement.

"Look at all this!" one of the volunteers exclaimed as Pete opened the van doors to reveal the mountain of boxes. "You've outdone yourselves this year."

Ruby beamed. "It's all Mr Baldwick's doing. He's the mastermind behind this."

The unloading got underway, and within moments, the reception area was filled with crates of tinned food, soft blankets, and toys.

I knelt beside Benji, stroking his soft fur, and gave Tiberius a reassuring belly rub. It felt good to do something so positive and was a welcome break from the tragedy at the Swan Tavern.

As the last of the boxes were unloaded and the volunteers began organising the supplies, Ruby and I stood back, watching the joyful chaos unfold. The dogs would be well taken care of, thanks to the generosity of the community.

After providing Pete with refreshments, he was on his way, and the dogs' home turned into delightful bedlam. Everywhere I looked, volunteers were rushing about, handing out treats and unfolding blankets, while overseeing the dogs as they were brought into the exercise area to join in the fun.

The dogs, sensing the festive atmosphere, were barking and wagging their tails in pure excitement. A scruffy terrier named Rusty was darting between people's legs, chasing after toys, while the older dogs, like my own Benji, lounged contentedly on new blankets, watching the commotion with a sleepy satisfaction.

"Look at them all." Ruby stood beside me, holding a cup of tea in one hand and a tiny pug under one arm. "If only Christmas could last all year for these little ones."

Molly Banbury, the dogs' home receptionist, joined us. She was a robust fifty with tight ginger curls, held partly under control by the eyepatch she wore. She passed me a cup of tea and a mince pie. "You've done a wonderful thing here, Veronica."

"The whole community came together to make this happen." I took a sip of tea and decided to broach a subject that had been on my mind ever since my holiday to Margate. "There are so many dogs outside of London who need homes, and there aren't the facilities to take them in."

"You're not wrong there. We do what we can locally, but we always need more space and more funds," Molly said.

"Perhaps we could open a site in Margate."

Her eyes widened. "Margate, you say? Why that area?"

"I'm opening an office in the county, and heard there was a need for a place for stray animals. While I'm down there getting my own matters in order, I can keep an eye on things. Or help with setting things up. Do you think the trustees would consider a new location for a shelter?"

"I know it's been talked about. And I have family down that way, so I can already think of a few people who'd be willing to volunteer. And there's a woman I know who runs a boarding kennel out that way, too. She's always trying to do more for the strays."

"Perhaps it's something for us to pursue in the new year?"

"I'll be right behind you." Molly smiled broadly. "We'll get those trustees into action. A new dogs' home! How exciting."

Ruby fed Benji and Tiberius a sausage. "I can already picture Battersea-on-Sea. I hope we make it happen. It's good to have plans for the future."

"It would be amazing, wouldn't it? Reaching out to more places, helping more dogs. Maybe even expanding beyond Margate someday," I said.

"Count me in. And now I'm a committed single lady, you have me at your disposal," Ruby said.

I arched an eyebrow. "How long will that last?"

"Forever. It's just me and ... you. The two of us. And of course, Benji."

I looked around at the happy mess and let out a soft sigh. "If only all problems were this easy to solve. Dogs never make things complicated. It's only ever people who stir up trouble."

Ruby raised her cup of tea in a mock toast. "Here's to dogs. And to meeting fewer complicated people."

I laughed and clinked my cup against hers. In that moment, surrounded by the warm, joyful noise of happy dogs and kind-hearted people, I wished more than anything that life could always be this simple.

But an unsolved murder awaited us at the Swan Tavern. And we had questions that needed answering.

# Chapter 13

I'd been reluctant to leave the welcoming warmth of the dogs' home, but we had to return to the scene of the crime. And when we arrived, the welcome was frosty. The moment we stepped into the hallway, Inspector Harold Finchley accosted us, his expression tight.

"Where have you ladies been?"

"Good day to you," I said. "We realised you'd be busy conducting thorough interviews with everyone, so we knew we'd have plenty of time to go about our own business."

"What business would that be?" he snapped. "You were most insistent we dig into matters, yet the second we do, you vanish. Some might call that suspicious."

"Then they would be idiots." I removed my hat, coat, and boots, and Baxter appeared and whisked them away.

Ruby nudged me and gave me a warning look, cautioning me not to irritate Inspector Finchley too fiercely.

"I'm glad to hear you're looking so objectively at this case," I said, as pleasantly as I could muster.

Inspector Finchley glanced down at Benji and Tiberius, who were sitting obediently by my side. "They need to go outside."

"Oh, dear," Ruby said, knowing the blast I'd unleash on the dim-witted inspector for making such a foolish assertion.

"It's snowing again! It would be unkind to leave them in the cold. You're not an unkind man, are you, Inspector?"

"I have allergies." As if to demonstrate, he let out an enormous sneeze, failing to cover it with either a handkerchief or hand.

Ruby tutted as she eased off her shoes. "Really! You don't want to be passing a cold around at Christmas. Nobody wants a gift like that."

"It's not a cold," he grumbled. "I'm telling you, I have dreadful allergies. I'm allergic to those dogs."

"Then you'd better be quick with questioning me, hadn't you. Shall we?" I walked away, hearing Ruby chortle as Inspector Finchley tutted and grumbled. I was making no allowances for the man, since he'd been of no help to me so far.

On the way into the sitting room, I paused by Mitzi, who gave me a knowing look. "How was the interview?"

"Brief," she said in a low voice. "The inspector ate three slices of cake while waiting for you to return."

"No conferring, if you please," Inspector Finchley said, catching us up. "As Miss Vale has repeatedly pointed out, this is still an open investigation."

"Quite right." I winked at Mitzi. I'd speak to her after my interview to see just how ineffective Inspector Finchley had been.

"I'll get Baxter started on the hot cocoa," she whispered, before hurrying away.

I settled myself in a chair in the sitting room, Benji on one side and Tiberius on the other. Inspector Finchley glowered at the dogs, making a point of sniffing several times, quite rudely. He remained standing. I recognised an intimidation tactic when I saw one. Sergeant Brown was stationed in one corner of the room.

"I'm asking you all the same questions," Inspector Finchley said. "I want to get the lay of the land, so to speak."

"Excellent work. I'll be happy to answer all queries," I replied.

He strode the length of the room and back again. "What was your relationship with Mr Robinson?"

"He was a new acquaintance," I said. "I met him for the first time at Mitzi's pre-Christmas gathering. She told me he was a new resident in Little Kennington."

"Mrs Draper said you own this tavern. Is that correct?"

"It's a family business," I said. "My late father purchased a number of pubs. When he passed, the business came to me."

"It's not the sort of business typical for a lady to own," Inspector Finchley said.

"In these modern times, what a lady can do is quite remarkable, don't you think?"

He grumbled a response that I didn't catch. I expected it hadn't been a compliment as to my business acumen.

"Did you talk to Mr Robinson at the party?" he asked.

"We had a brief conversation or two," I said. "He was involved with the party games and dancing."

"That wasn't your sort of thing?"

"I joined in. It was a fun evening, although crowded."

Inspector Finchley sniffled again. "What were your conversations about?"

"Mainly Mr Robinson's manners. He'd left them at the door when he joined the party."

"So, you didn't like the man?"

"I barely knew him, but our brief acquaintance wasn't positive," I said. "I suggest you speak to my landlady, Aggie."

"Was she at this party, too?"

"No, but Mr Robinson went into the public bar during the party," I explained. "Aggie has encountered him on numerous occasions. It appears he's very fond of drink, but not of paying his bill."

"Which would be unfortunate for you, since this pub is your concern. Were you losing money because of his lack of funds?"

I was surprised Inspector Finchley was considering such a possibility. Perhaps my opinion of him had been too harsh. "Aggie stands for no nonsense. We don't allow tabs in the pub because it causes problems."

"Why were you in the public bar?" he asked.

"To speak to Aggie and ensure all was well," I said. "And this will be of interest to you. While I was there, Mr Robinson had a disagreement with a man called Nathan. It was something to do with money. I suggest you speak to this Nathan and find out more. Nathan Dunmow."

"Was this fellow also at the Draper's party?"

"No, he'd dropped into the public bar for a drink," I said. "Their conversation was tense."

So far, Inspector Finchley had made no notes, and while his sergeant stood in the corner of the room, he hadn't jotted down a single thing either. Were they not taking these interviews seriously?

"Other than meeting Mr Robinson at the pre-Christmas gathering, you'd had no contact with him?" Inspector Finchley asked.

"That is correct." Were we about to go round in an infuriating circle? I'd have to put my foot down if that was the case.

"And other than some brief conversations, when you thought little of his character, that was the only time you spent with Mr Robinson?"

"No. We had breakfast together the next morning and then we all went skating together."

Inspector Finchley finally pulled out a notepad and flicked it open. "Ah, yes. Skating in Poplar Park, and then back here. That was when you found Mr Robinson after his accident."

"No, I didn't find him first. My dog, Benji, smelled something was wrong. He raced ahead with Tiberius, and they discovered Mr Robinson dead in the snow. And it looked far from an accident to me."

"Does your mind often turn to dark thoughts?" Inspector Finchley asked. "Colonel Draper mentioned you did something in the war. I don't agree with females serving. They're too fragile."

"I assure you, my temperament is the opposite of fragile."

"Even so, you returned to a different world."

"A better world," I said sharply. "But my service during the war has nothing to do with this situation."

"A fragile feminine mind is nothing to be ashamed of," Inspector Finchley said. "But it now makes sense to me why you'd instantly consider Mr Robinson's accident was something else."

I clenched my hands and took a few seconds to breathe deeply. He was suggesting I'd taken leave of my senses because I was a woman. I was determined to maintain my composure despite my rising irritation, and I remained silent for fear my tongue would lash out.

"We all have our limits, don't we, Miss Vale? I'm simply trying to understand how your experiences have coloured your judgement. Did you nurse? Saw plenty of wounded men, no doubt."

"I'm not a nurse, and my judgement is just fine." My voice was clipped. "And while you're busy questioning my mental state, a man is still dead, and your investigation is going nowhere."

"Now, now, my dear lady." He waved a hand dismissively, his tone condescending. "There's no need to get emotional."

"I'm not emotional, Inspector, I'm factual. There's a difference. And if you'd stop sneezing for five minutes, you might be able to hear what I'm saying."

He sneezed as if on cue, and didn't bother to apologise. "I've been in this line of work for years. I know when something is a simple accident, and when there's more to it."

"And you think John's death was a simple accident?"

"That's what it looks like."

"To anyone paying attention to the clues, it's clear something's wrong."

His eyes narrowed. "Are you saying I don't know how to do my job?"

"If listening is part of your job, then you, sir, are failing. You've already made up your mind, haven't you? Mr Robinson's death was just an unfortunate accident, case closed, so you can go home and put your feet up."

Inspector Finchley raised a hand to stop me, then sneezed heartily again, shaking his head. "This is getting us nowhere. You're too irrational to speak to. We're done here."

I stood, unable to contain my exasperation. "You're dismissing me? Without even taking anything I've said seriously?"

"I'll take your comments into account. Now, if you'll excuse me, I need to call in your friend. Perhaps she'll be less combative."

I nearly laughed at the absurdity of it. Ruby Smythe never backed down from a fight, even while she fluttered her eyelashes.

"Miss Smythe," he called towards the door.

Ruby appeared in the doorway, eyebrows raised at the sight of Inspector Finchley's watery eyes and flushed face. "Oh, dear, I hope Veronica hasn't made you cry."

He sniffed again. "It's these cursed dogs."

Ruby glanced at me, suppressing a smirk.

"Please, Miss Smythe, take a seat." Inspector Finchley gestured to the chair I'd just vacated.

I shot Ruby a look before turning on my heel, my patience well and truly gone. I stepped into the hallway, closing the door behind me with more force than necessary.

The audacity of that man, dismissing me as though I were some hysterical woman who didn't know her own mind. I took a deep breath, trying to calm the simmering anger in my chest.

Mitzie stood by the window at the entrance door, her arms folded as she watched the snowfall outside. When she heard me, she turned, a concerned look on her face. "Well?"

"He's utterly useless." I tried to keep my voice steady. "Inspector Finchley has already decided John's death was an accident."

Mitzie's mouth tightened into a thin line. "He was the same with me. A few questions, nothing too probing. I thought he'd be more thorough, but he's dismissing it all as a mishap."

I rubbed my temples, feeling the tension build. "I need to learn more about John. Did he have a house in Little Kennington?"

"He was in lodgings. I know the landlady. Mrs May Bell. She's a funny old sort, but sweet in her own way. She lives close to the village pond. She's a widower, so uses the spare rooms to make ends meet."

"Do you know her address?"

"Of course. I know everyone in Little Kennington. It's a vital role as lady of the manor." She tinkled a laugh.

"I should speak to her. She might know something. Anything could be useful at this point."

"Poor May. She'll be so upset to know one of her lodgers is dead. I think John was the only one staying with her at the moment."

I looked at the telephone, wondering if I'd have more luck this time. "I'll telephone her now if the line is operational and arrange something."

"Good luck with that. Eddie tried ten minutes ago and he couldn't get a peep. The service keeps coming and going."

I walked to the telephone, giving it a quick jiggle before picking up the receiver. For a moment, I heard nothing but the usual hiss of static, and then—clear as day—the dial tone hummed in my ear. "Hooray! We're back in business."

She clapped her hands together. "Finally! You'll call Jacob, then?"

I hesitated. "I should, but no. This investigation comes first. I'll speak to Mrs Bell. Jacob will have to wait." Even as I said it, a small part of me ached to hear his voice. But there were bigger matters at hand. And if I didn't act quickly, we'd lose valuable time.

I contacted the operator and was put through to Mrs Bell. The line clicked and buzzed. I hoped it would hold out. One ring. Two. Then a voice answered. "Little Kennington 4598. May Bell speaking."

"Mrs Bell, this is Veronica Vale. I'm a friend of Mrs Mitzie Draper."

"Is that so? She was good enough to send me a Christmas hamper. She does it every year."

"She's kind like that. I'm sorry to trouble you, but Mitzie informed me you know John Robinson. He rents a room from you, doesn't he?"

There was a pause, followed by a wary, "He does. What's this about?"

"There's no pleasant way to tell you this, but John is no longer with us. He died."

Mrs Bell inhaled sharply. "Good lord! What happened? I thought he was spending Christmas with the Drapers."

"He was. I found him with a serious head injury, close to where we're staying," I said.

She blew out a breath. "Well, I never."

"I need to ask you a few things about him, if you wouldn't mind. May I come by this afternoon?"

Mrs Bell hesitated, and I could almost hear her weighing the options. "I've got nothing better to do, and there's sherry and some mince pies that need eating. But watch the roads out this way, they're ... and don't use the ... road."

"Sorry, Mrs Bell. You're breaking up. Could you repeat that?"

"The ... road."

The line went dead.

"Drat!" I muttered, giving the receiver a few firm taps. "Mrs Bell? If you can still hear me, I'll be there shortly."

The line remained silent.

Mitzie raised an eyebrow. "Are you really going out on Christmas Eve? The conditions have only got worse since your last escape. I was most surprised when I couldn't find you. Baxter said you slipped out with Ruby when the interviews began."

"Such as they are. And we were escaping for good reason. The dogs needed their Christmas party, and I never miss it."

"Oh! I forgot all about your wonderful party. How smashing. I'm glad you made it there and back safely."

"And with plenty of gifts." I checked the telephone one last time and set it back in its cradle. Thwarted again by the weather.

"Chin up, old girl. It'll be up and running again soon. And if Jacob is the one for you, he won't mind a little tangle in your romance," Mitzie teased lightly. "Although he must be missing you."

I had been thinking about Jacob, but I wouldn't be distracted by romantic nonsense. "That's quite enough of that. This investigation comes first. Let's find out what Mrs Bell knows. And maybe this time, we'll make progress in uncovering exactly what happened to John."

# Chapter 14

After Ruby had been interviewed by Inspector Finchley, and I used that term lightly, I told her of the plan to speak to John's landlady. We were figuring out the logistics when Aggie bustled into the sitting room.

"Sorry to disturb you, but I thought you should know, Nathan is in the bar. You told me to look out for him."

"Thank you, Aggie." I set my coat to one side.

"He's pleading poverty, so you may convince him to talk if you buy him a few drinks. He never stays long, though, so you need to move sharpish," Aggie said.

"What about our visit to see Mrs Bell?" Ruby asked.

"If we're quick, we'll still have time to visit her. But this may be the only opportunity to question Nathan," I said.

"Nathan usually comes in every evening after work, but I've not seen him since his argument with John," Aggie said.

"There could be a good reason for that," I said.

She arched an eyebrow. "Will there be trouble? Should I get the bat ready?"

"No need. I'm sure Nathan will behave."

"Bat?" Ruby asked.

"Knock someone on the head and they soon see sense." Aggie chuckled as she led us to the bar. "Although I've never needed to use it on Nathan. He's a simple man. And I've never seen him angry with anyone until he argued with John."

As I entered the public bar, the warmth hit me, along with the familiar smell of beer and smoke. The Swan Tavern bar was busy as people relaxed and began their festive merriment. With Christmas Eve on our doorstep, it was no wonder there were so many smiling faces.

"There he is." I nodded towards the far end of the bar where Nathan sat hunched over his drink. He wore a heavy coat, a cap pulled low over his brow, suggesting he wasn't in the mood for pleasant conversation.

As Ruby and I approached Nathan, he slid a glance our way. The furrow of his brow deepened as we came closer and he realised we were focused on him.

"Good evening, Nathan." My tone was friendly but firm. He glanced at me, then at Ruby, but said nothing. I didn't let a little ill humour deter me. "Do you mind if we join you?"

He hesitated. "I'm not good company."

I sat down next to him and Ruby took the stool on his other side.

Nathan gave us a wary look. "I don't know either of you. And you're not friends with my wife."

I nodded at Aggie to bring over the drinks. "But you may know my name if you've ever read the licensee sign above the door. I'm Veronica Vale, and this is my friend, Ruby."

At the mention of my surname, Nathan's expression changed. His eyes darted to the bar, where Aggie was preparing our drinks. He seemed to consider his options for a moment.

"And as the owner of the pub, I could offer you a free drink."

"That's good of you, but why would you do that?" he asked.

Aggie strode over with our drinks. A pint of ale for Nathan, a martini for Ruby, and a gin fizz for me. "Nathan, I hope you're behaving in such esteemed company."

"You're friends with these ladies?" he asked.

Aggie gave him his pint. "Miss Vale is an excellent employer, and she works as hard as her father to ensure the Swan Tavern thrives, so be polite to her."

"That's kind of you to say." The mention of my father almost distracted me. "He had a soft spot for this tavern."

Nathan relaxed as he reached for the pint. "I trust Aggie. If she thinks you're trustworthy, then I have no issue. And thanks for the drink."

"You're welcome."

"They just want to talk," Aggie said. "There's nothing to worry about."

Nathan grumbled something under his breath, but Aggie's vouching seemed to loosen the tension in his shoulders. He leaned back slightly, though his eyes were still watchful.

He took a long, slow drink before setting it down with a thud. "What's this about, then?"

"We're looking into what happened to John Robinson." I watched him closely. His reaction was subtle, just the briefest flicker of something in his eyes, but it told me he'd heard about John's death.

"What about him?" Nathan's voice was flat, guarded.

"Do you know what happened to him?"

"I heard he took a tumble outside. He was most likely drunk. He usually is."

"I was here when you had a disagreement with him. Something about money he'd taken that you needed back?"

Nathan froze for a second, his pint halfway to his mouth. He lowered it slowly, his lips tightening. "Why is that important?"

"Be nice, Nathan." Aggie had stayed within earshot. "If you're agreeable to these ladies, I might find a whisky chaser to go along with that pint."

He scowled, clearly unhappy with the direction of the conversation. "It was nothing. A squabble over money."

"Considering what happened to John, I'd say it was far from nothing," I said.

"He fell and hit his head, didn't he?" Nathan asked.

"We don't think it was an accident," I said.

Nathan seemed genuinely shocked. "How would you know that? Were you there when it happened?"

"We found John," Ruby said. "He was skating with us but left the ice. When we returned to the tavern, we discovered his body. As you can imagine, we were shocked."

Nathan shifted uncomfortably, his fingers tightening around his pint. "I'm sorry you had to see that. That must have been unpleasant."

"It was. But we want to know what happened to him. If it wasn't a fall, then someone injured John," I said.

Recognition dawned in Nathan's eyes. "Our argument wasn't that serious! John owed me some money, and he wasn't keen on paying up. But it wasn't enough to kill over."

"From what I overheard, John left you in financial strife. You thought he was helping you, but it was a trick, wasn't it?" I asked.

Nathan fidgeted with his pint, not making eye contact. "I was a fool. I put my money into John's betting ring. He said it was a sure thing, and he guaranteed I'd triple my money. The timing was perfect. I wanted to give my family a Christmas they'd never forget. They'll remember this one, but for all the wrong reasons." He let out a bitter laugh, rubbing a hand over his face. "What a damn idiot I've been. No money for gifts or food."

Ruby and I exchanged a glance, and I felt a twinge of pity for the man. Nathan was rough around the edges, but there was something sad about the way his shoulders slumped under the weight of his mistake.

"How much did you lose?" I asked gently.

"More than I can make up, even with taking extra shifts at the factory." Nathan's voice was thick with regret. "I haven't told the wife yet. She'll be mad. Christmas is ruined, and the children will go without. It'll break my heart to see their sad faces."

There was a heavy pause. It was easy to see the situation for what it was. A man trying to dig himself out of a hole he'd fallen into, and too proud or too scared to ask for help.

Nathan appeared to gather himself. "If this was murder, why aren't the police investigating?"

"They are. But we've had trouble getting them to take our concerns seriously," I said.

"Which is why we're in charge." Ruby lifted her drink in a cheers motion, but didn't take a sip.

"Are you experts? Police?"

"No, but we've seen plenty of trouble and know how to handle situations such as this," I said. "Nathan, could you let us know where you were on the afternoon John died?"

Nathan stiffened, his eyes darting to mine, wide with alarm. "No, I didn't do it! I swear on my life. On my children's lives. And I can prove it."

"I'd be interested in that proof," I said.

He checked the time. "I'll have to show you. If you come with me, you'll see I'm innocent, but we need to leave now."

"Where are we going?"

Nathan downed his pint and stood. "To the park."

I glanced at Ruby, and she shrugged. We had nothing to lose by hearing him out.

Aggie, who'd been watching from the bar, stepped over. "I trust Nathan. He's not perfect, but you won't find yourself in any trouble if you go with him. And I have a good idea what he wants to show you."

Just in case we were walking into trouble, I collected Benji and Tiberius as backup, and then stepped out of the pub and into the frigid evening air. Outside, the snow was falling lightly, dusting the streets with a sparkling, festive layer. Benji and Tiberius trotted beside us, their breath puffing in the chilly air as Nathan led us along the busy street.

We walked in silence, the snow crunching underfoot, the air crisp and still. After a short while, we turned off the street and entered the park, passing by open wrought-iron gates.

Nathan hurried towards a vast wooden shed with a short queue of children waiting outside with several bundled-up adults in thick winter coats. The sign over the door to the shed read: Christmas Fairyland.

"What's this all about?" I asked.

Nathan stopped at the entrance, motioning for us to wait. "If the big shops can have a grotto, so can we. And we're doing it for a good cause. Give me five minutes. Don't come inside until I'm ready." He cupped his hands and breathed into them. "I shouldn't have had that pint."

"Here. These will help." I passed him a small paper bag of mints.

He nodded a thanks and disappeared inside before we could ask any more questions.

Ruby rubbed her arms to fend off the cold. "You don't think he's making a run for it, do you?"

I examined the shed. "There's no way out the back. I've never seen a grotto outside of a department store. This is impressive." There were lanterns and candles, decorations, and even a tree standing outside.

"What does this prove about his innocence?" Ruby asked.

"Let's give Nathan a chance to explain. If he doesn't come out soon, though, we'll have to tackle him. We need to get to Mrs Bell before the snow gets any heavier."

After a few minutes, Nathan emerged. He wore a red suit, complete with a large black belt, white-trimmed gloves, and a bright, oversized hat.

Ruby snorted, trying to suppress her laughter, and I couldn't help but smile at the sight. Nathan looked almost bashful as he shifted in the outfit, tugging at the hat as if to make sure it sat just right.

"I do this shift when I'm not working," he explained, his voice gruff but with a hint of pride. "It's for the local children's homes. Come in and see what we do. This is where I was when John met his ... well, you know." He glanced at the children, clearly not wanting to mention murder in front of them.

Inside the grotto, another small group of bright-eyed children, bundled up in scarves and gloves, lined up eagerly as they waited to meet Father Christmas. The grotto was decorated with sparkling tinsel, ornaments, and a large, festively adorned chair at the centre, which must be Nathan's throne.

He took his place in the chair, settling in as the first child approached, looking up at him with awe. Nathan leaned down, speaking softly to the little one, his gruff exterior melting away as he slipped into his role. He handed over a small wrapped gift, the child's face lighting up as she scampered back to the waiting adult.

I was about to comment on how different Nathan seemed when Benji darted forward. Before anyone could stop him, he leapt onto Nathan's lap, wagging his tail as if he'd been waiting all night for his turn with Father Christmas, and couldn't wait a second longer. He grabbed Nathan's false white beard and gently tugged it.

Nathan froze, his eyes widening in surprise, and for a second, the grotto went silent, until Ruby burst out laughing. I joined in, unable to hold back, and soon, the children were laughing, too.

"Benji's been good this year and deserves a gift," I said.

"As if you had any doubt." Ruby patted Tiberius. "Would you like a turn?"

My foster dog didn't seem so keen, and watched as Nathan grumbled under his breath, but there was a bemused smile on his bearded face as he gently patted Benji's head.

I gently coaxed Benji off Nathan's lap, so he could resume his Father Christmas duties, and avoid getting his beard chewed on. Ruby and I watched from the edge of the grotto as the warm, magical glow of the holiday spirit filled the air.

A lady dressed as Mother Christmas helped a child outside with their gift and then joined us. "Which ones are yours?"

"Oh! None of them. Well, Benji and Tiberius are a part of my family," I said. "We just came to see Nathan in action."

She smiled. "He's so good with the children. Many of them have had a bad start in life, but he's so patient with them and they always leave with a smile on their faces. Nathan helps us to restore the magic of Christmas."

"How often does he volunteer?" I asked.

"As often as possible. This is his third shift this week. He's usually here in the afternoons, and even changes his factory shifts so he can be here at the busiest time. We have an arrangement with a dozen children's homes, so we're always busy. Nathan also helps us collect toys and donations throughout the year, so we never run out of gifts."

"I'm happy we could witness your good work," I said.

The woman nodded and hurried off to help a child who clutched their small gift, looking a little overwhelmed.

This wasn't how I'd expected our questioning to go, but I was thrilled to find Nathan had such a benevolent spirit.

There was a short pause as the next group of children filed in, so I used it to tiptoe to Nathan's side. "What a wonderful thing you're doing."

He adjusted his beard. "I didn't like John, but I spend my time doing good, not harm. I have dozens of children who will tell you that."

"Mother Christmas has already done that," Ruby said. "Well done. This is excellent."

A flush splashed across Nathan's cheeks. "I do what I can. I hope you catch whoever did this to John. He wasn't a good man, but we all have our struggles. Some of us cope, while others don't make it through. He didn't deserve to die."

We stepped back as the next child approached, and left the delightful grotto, making our way back to the Swan Tavern, and leaving Nathan to his worthy cause.

"Nathan didn't kill John." Ruby hugged herself as the snow fluttered down around us.

"His alibi is solid," I said. "Which means we focus back on our own party of suspects. It's got to be someone we already know. Someone we've already questioned."

Ruby glanced at the sky. "Is there still time to speak to Mrs Bell?"

I nodded. "Let's see if she knows of any secrets John was keeping. A secret that led to his death."

# Chapter 15

"You want to get there as quickly as possible, don't you?" Ruby asked. "My car will whizz us to Little Kennington and back in a jiffy. And the sooner we go, the less likely we are to get asked any awkward questions, especially from Eddie. If his mood grows any more sour, he may shut us in the shed with the swan and force us to spend Christmas Day in the cold."

I stood by the window in the sitting room after our return from the grotto. As we'd walked back, the snow had started pelting down, and was now so fast, all I could see were blobs of white and my own reflection. "I'm not sure driving is such a good idea. We could try public transport."

"That won't be any faster! I can drive anything, no matter the terrain or the conditions," Ruby assured me. "You've seen me do it. Trust me."

It wasn't that I doubted Ruby's competence behind the wheel, but after having a near miss on our way here, and with the conditions much worse than when we arrived, I was reluctant to put my life in her hands.

"This is the quickest and simplest way to get us to Little Kennington to speak to Mrs Bell. And she's expecting us. It would be impolite if we stood her up."

I checked the time. If we left it any later, we'd be driving back in the darkness, a sure path to an icy end. "Very well. I'll leave Tiberius here, though. He wasn't enjoying the snow when we walked back from the park. Baxter will take care of him. Benji will accompany us, since he's an excellent scent hound, so will hunt out any clues John may have left behind."

Ruby clasped her hands together. "I'm excited to test the car's limits in the snow."

I glowered at her. "We'll go slow and steady, or we'll return to spend the holidays as the Ghosts of Christmas Buffoons."

After dressing in our warmest clothes and sneaking out of the tavern to avoid Eddie and Inspector Finchley, who were having a brandy in the billiard room, rather than solving this case, we made our way to Ruby's car. We spent a moment clearing the snow and then climbed inside. It felt like an icebox.

"We'll defrost once the engine has heated," Ruby said. "We just need to give her a moment. Are you warm in the back, Benji?"

Benji woofed softly, already snuggling under a blanket put there especially for the dogs.

We didn't dare sit for too long, though, in case someone heard the engine start and peeked out to see what was going on, so Ruby expertly manoeuvred her car along the passage and onto the main road.

"It's almost clear of snow," she exclaimed. "I knew they'd be keeping the streets safe to avoid any trouble so close to Christmas."

"I'm glad we're investigating this avenue. After hitting an incompetent policeman and Eddie roadblock regarding John, we have no choice but to take matters into our own hands," I said. "Questioning Nathan led us along a dead end, so we desperately need to make progress. We're running out of time."

Ruby kept a steady, safe pace as we drove along the London streets. Even the terrible weather wasn't keeping people inside. The shopfronts were alive with a dazzling array of colours and lights, creating a festive feel that showcased winter wonderlands complete with toy soldiers, ice-skating figurines, and beautifully dressed mannequins in their Christmas finest.

"Look at those brave souls!" Ruby pointed to a small group of bundled-up carol singers standing beneath a streetlamp. "It looks like they're collecting for charity."

"We should do that for the dogs' home," I said.

"As much as I love the adorable strays you take under your wing, I have my limits, and standing on a frozen street corner to gather a few pennies is one of them. We did our bit with the meat and the Christmas party. I still smile when I remember all those happy furry faces."

It made me smile, too. Ruby was a generous benefactor to the dogs' home, as was I, although I donated my time more often than she did. We supported in our own ways, and the dogs were always grateful.

"Just a moment," I said. "That must be the tobacconist's shop Eddie and Mitzie visited. Pull over."

"But you don't smoke!"

"I never took to the habit, but I want to double-check their alibis. I'll be two minutes," I assured her.

"If they've got any chocolate mints, get me a bag." Ruby handed over some money.

I opened the car door, narrowly avoiding stepping into a heap of snow. I pulled my coat around me and hurried into the shop. There was a gentleman waiting to be served, but he only took a moment to make his purchase, and then I had the place to myself.

"What will it be, miss?" the shopkeeper asked.

"A dozen chocolate mints, please. And if you'd be so kind, an answer to a question."

He placed Ruby's mints into a small brown paper bag and handed them over. "The first request is simple. What question do you have for me?"

"Do you know Colonel Edward Draper?" I asked.

"Indeed, I do. A fine fellow. He doesn't visit as often as I'd like, but I always welcome his patronage. We sometimes play bowls together when I visit my sister in Little Kennington."

"Was he in here recently with his wife?"

The shopkeeper handed back my change, his eyes slightly narrowed. "Is there trouble?"

"No trouble. They're friends of mine, and I was interested in the type of tobacco Colonel Draper bought. I'm thinking of making some last-minute gift purchases."

"A very good choice, miss. His wife favours the cigarillos, and we supply attractive carry cases. They make popular gifts at this time of year."

"They were in here recently?" I asked again.

"They were. It's the first time I've seen them in over a month. I sold them a box of cigarillos and some Players. Would you like to try some? We have some exotic flavours. And why not sample the cases? They're beautifully designed. The perfect gift for the discerning cigarillo smoker."

I had wondered about buying something else for Mitzie, since she'd been such a generous hostess, so selected a pretty blue enamelled case, and had it wrapped.

With my questions happily answered and my dear friends in the clear, I hurried back into the snow and was grateful to slide into Ruby's car, which had warmed up considerably from its previous icebox incarnation. "Mitzie and Eddie weren't involved in John's murder. And I have an extra gift for Mitzie."

"I knew they couldn't have anything to do with this dreadful business. For all his curmudgeonly nature, Eddie is a giant moustached teddy bear." Ruby eased the car back into the traffic. "And Mitzie is too sweet to even injure a fly!"

"I couldn't let our friendship cloud my judgement. Not when Eddie has been so bull-headed about the John situation, resisting the possibility of murder. He's smarter than that."

"Stubbornness sometimes bests smart. Although our knowledge of Eddie should have convinced us as to his innocence."

"What knowledge would that be?" I slid a chocolate mint from the bag and popped it into my mouth.

"I always imagined Eddie being as forthright with his method of murder as he is with his comments on social situations he disapproves of," Ruby said.

"Oh! A bullet right between the eyes, you mean?" I asked.

"Exactly! The murder doesn't fit his modus operandi."

Ruby had a point. Eddie had been a career soldier, gaining his stripes through hard work and active duty. He'd consider leaving a man for dead in the snow a cowardly way to end a life.

As we left behind the glittering London streets and hectic buzz of Christmas excitement, the roads became narrower and slippery, the car's headlamps highlighting the snow that showed no sign of stopping. If anything, it was getting worse.

"From what you told me, Mrs Bell didn't sound shocked about what happened to John," Ruby said.

"I expect she had the measure of the man. She must have witnessed John's comings and goings and heard his exaggerated claims of wartime heroism," I said. "From what Mitzie told me about Mrs Bell, she's not to be trifled with, so I can't imagine she tolerates liars."

"We'll soon see what she's made of," Ruby said. "In ten minutes, we'll be at her door."

"And finally warm. I hope she offers us tea. I'm parched."

"I'd prefer sherry."

"If it's from Mitzi's hamper, it'll be excellent quality."

There was barely any traffic now, for which I was grateful, as the road ahead of us was white.

"It's really coming down," Ruby observed as snow pelted against the windscreen.

"And more heavy snow is forecast," I said. "We won't get to see my mother and Matthew on Christmas Day. Not if we get snowed in."

"Your mother will understand. And she won't be lonely, since she has all those cats to care for." Ruby squeaked and gripped the steering wheel tighter.

"Is anything wrong?" I hadn't missed the car's rear end slide.

"No! I'm in full control. Sing me a carol to take my mind off things."

"Things! Like the car misbehaving?"

"This isn't misbehaving, this is … testing limits." Ruby patted the dashboard.

I fell silent, ensuring Ruby had her full attention on the whited-out road. The farther we got from the Swan Tavern, the less frequently streetlamps appeared, leaving us with only the headlamps to guide us into Little Kennington. The snow fell in thick, relentless sheets, transforming the countryside into an unfamiliar landscape.

Ruby leaned forward, her knuckles white on the steering wheel as she squinted through the windscreen. The wipers struggled valiantly against the onslaught, barely managing to clear the glass before a fresh layer of snow obscured our view once more.

Trees loomed on either side of the road, their bare branches stretching out like grasping fingers. I shivered, pulling my coat tighter around me. The car's tires crunched through the deepening snow, and every so often, a gust of wind would shake the vehicle, causing Ruby to tighten her grip and adjust our course with practiced precision. She really was an excellent driver.

Neither of us spoke, but I sensed Ruby's growing unease matching my own. This journey had been unwise, but it was too late to turn back.

A flicker of movement caught my eye, and I instinctively pressed back against the seat. "Ruby," I whispered, not wanting to startle her. "Did you see that?"

She shook her head, her eyes never leaving the road. "What was it?"

I peered into the gloom, straining to catch another glimpse of whatever had darted through the trees. "I'm not sure. It was probably nothing, just the snow playing tricks on—"

A low growl from the backseat cut me off. Benji was on high alert, his ears pricked forward and his body tense. He moved to the edge of his seat, nose pressed against the window, a continuous rumble emanating from his chest.

"What's got into him?" Ruby kept her attention on the road.

I turned in my seat, reaching back to calm Benji. His fur stood on end beneath my fingers.

Benji let out a sharp bark that made Ruby and me jump. The car swerved slightly before Ruby corrected our course.

"Shh, it's fine, boy," I soothed, but my words sounded hollow. Benji's behaviour only reinforced the building sense of unease.

I returned my attention to the road ahead, scanning the treeline for any sign of movement. The snow formed shapes in the darkness. Was that a person standing by that gnarled oak? No, just a trick of the light and shadow. I was making myself unnecessarily fretful.

Then I saw it again. A shape darting between the trees, keeping pace with our slow-moving car. My heart rate quickened. "Ruby, I think there's something out there. Something following us."

Ruby's jaw tightened. "You could be going snow blind. Those lovely eyes of yours aren't as sharp as they used to be."

"How very dare you," I murmured.

Ruby shot me a brief smile. "It's not far now. Do you see the sign?"

The headlights illuminated a road sign ahead, partially obscured by snow: Little Kennington: one mile.

I took a deep breath. "I think I can see lights. That must be the village!"

Benji, his head resting on my shoulder, let out a sigh and a gentle whine, his tail thumping, and his tension fading. Whatever had startled him was gone.

"If you want to romp in the snow, I'll need to fit you out with winter boots and a scarf," I said.

"I could knit Benji something adorable to wear. Oh, no, I take that back. I always drop my stitches, and my designs look like the recipient requested three arm holes. You should get your mother to make him something," Ruby said. "She's an ace with the knitting needles."

I smiled and shook my head. My dear, infuriating mother feigned illness whenever anything was asked of her, but she always came through with what I needed at the right moment. And she'd already knitted Benji a fine scarf, which he'd worn for two days, and then torn on a thorn bush. It was his subtle way of saying he didn't need clothes. His thick coat was more than enough.

"This slow pace is torturous," Ruby said. "And my toes are numb. I'll speed up."

"Slow and steady, remember?" I squinted into the gloom. There was a large white pile of snow heaped in the middle of the road. Before I had a chance to warn Ruby to steer around it, the white heap unfurled, revealing enormous wings and an orange beak.

Ruby screamed, twisting the steering wheel hard to avoid hitting the swan, and spun the car. She righted the spin by steering into it, but the road was too slippery and the car kept turning, making me dizzy.

Benji barked his alarm as he found himself on an unexpected fairground ride.

"Down, boy. Stay down!" I said, unsure which direction we were headed.

"I've got this, I've got this! Although hold on to something, just in case I haven't," Ruby shouted.

I gripped the seat, unable to do anything to assist in our snowy slide towards who knew where. We had to stop soon.

"I'll let her keep spinning. I'm in control." Ruby's tone suggested she was anything but in control, but adding my panic to the situation wouldn't help matters.

"I trust you not to get us killed." I was proud of myself for not squeaking out my words of encouragement. In truth, I was terrified and more than a little queasy. And I was grateful we were the only ones on the road. Otherwise, this situation would have been much worse.

"Any second now, and I'll have her just where I want her." Ruby spoke through gritted teeth.

There was a bang as we slammed into a bank of snow. The car spun another half turn, and the nose pitched into a ditch.

# Chapter 16

I didn't move for several seconds, the shock of the car crash pinning me in my seat. It was only when my body involuntarily took in a huge breath that I realised nothing was broken. I kept my composure as I wiggled my fingers and toes. Everything worked. Nothing hurt.

"Ruby, are you injured?" I called out. "Benji?"

The inside of the car was gloomy, covered by a heavy blanket of snow from the snowbank we'd slid into, so I couldn't see if Ruby was conscious.

Benji gave a reassuring woof to let me know he was fine.

I fumbled around in the gloom until I found Ruby's arm. "Talk to me. Are you hurt?"

"I have the biggest bruise on my ego and possibly my hip. What a humiliation! My beloved car, stuck in a ditch. There must have been black ice hidden under the snow. I couldn't get her to behave, no matter what I did."

I breathed out a sigh of relief. "Better the car stuck than us dead."

"We'll get her going again. We just need to shove her out of the ditch and give her a push."

"I'm going nowhere for now. The snow has me trapped in on this side." I didn't bother to try my passenger door. Snow was all I could see from the window.

"You can climb out of this side. Give me a second to move and then you can wriggle over and get free." Ruby eased her door open, and a flurry of snow blasted in. She shivered but pushed on, regardless.

While Ruby squirmed out of the seat and through the small gap, I checked on Benji. He was unflappable, lying on the back seat just as I'd asked him to, his tail wagging. Once I was certain he was unharmed, I crawled over the seats and into the blizzard.

"Crikey! It's like an arctic freeze has set in. I'm all for a white Christmas, but this takes the biscuit." Ruby held onto the car as she slipped around to the front. "Oh! This is not what one wants to see. What a bother. It'll take more than my maintenance skills to right this situation. How ghastly."

I slid around to join her. One of the car's wheels was flat, and the headlight on my side was smashed. The front bumper had also dropped off.

"We're not far from Little Kennington," I said. "We can make it on foot if we don't dawdle."

"My coat will be ruined! This is new season winter wear. You know I've been saving for months to afford it." Ruby tugged the dark green woollen coat with its large black buttons tighter around her torso.

"We'll only make it worse by lingering. Step to it. Quick march, and we'll be at Mrs Bell's in twenty minutes. I saw lights just before we spun, so a warm house is close by."

Ruby grabbed her handbag from the car. "It was a swan on the road, wasn't it? Or did I hallucinate something large and white with an orange beak looming up at us?"

"I also saw a swan." I got Benji out of the car. I was worried about his paws in these icy conditions, but if we kept up a fast trot, none of us would freeze. "At first, I thought it was a pile of snow."

"The same here. What was a swan doing in the middle of the road in these wretched conditions?"

"It must be unwell." I hurried to the side of the road, using the spindly trees to provide a small amount of shelter. It took me a few seconds to get the right technique so I wouldn't fall, but then I was moving. "Or it could be pining for its mate, since it was alone. Swans mate for life."

"Oh! Here's an idea. Perhaps we have its injured companion in the tavern's shed." Ruby copied my movements. "The swan gave up the will to live and flopped onto the road to meet a grisly end."

"I doubt swans have that amount of forward planning."

"How about this? It wanted to take us out because we have its mate and it wants revenge. It thinks we've imprisoned its life partner." Ruby slid through the snow, shielding her eyes as the blizzard swirled around and soaked us, the cold biting deep and chilling me to the marrow.

"I don't think swans have such advanced reasoning as to plot revenge."

"That one did! It had a mean glint in its eyes."

"We were spinning so fast, you couldn't have seen its eyes!"

"It was up to something devious. And it's hiding now. It's probably watching and preparing for an attack," Ruby said.

"Then we'd better not linger, or the swan will put its nefarious ideas into practice."

Ruby looked around, seeking our feathered troublemaker, but the no doubt terrified bird was nowhere to be found. The poor creature wouldn't survive out here for long. I hoped it found shelter.

We established a fast rhythm of slide-marching as we headed towards the welcome lights of Little Kennington.

"We haven't had conditions like this in years," I said.

Ruby slowed and squinted through the blizzard. She grabbed my arm. "I see movement in the trees."

"It's the snow blowing around. Hurry! Or we really will freeze." I checked on Benji, who was having a high time of it, snapping at giant blobs of snow and racing around, more like a pup than a sensible adult dog.

"I'm telling you, there's someone out there. Hello! We could do with a hand. My car slid off the road, and we need to get to Little Kennington. Can you help us find the quickest route?" Ruby called out. "I say, can you hear me?"

There was no reply.

"The faster you walk, the quicker we'll get out of this blizzard and you'll stop hallucinating a snowman coming to our rescue." I looked over my shoulder, sensing movement, just as Ruby ducked and yelped. An enormous swan sailed over her head and crashed into the snowdrift on the opposite side of the road.

Ruby was flat on her face, almost buried by the snow. The attacking swan pulled itself out of the snowdrift, shook snow from its beak, and charged towards her, its wings outstretched.

"Ruby! Look out." I dashed closer with Benji by my side, both of us sliding and unable to get a grip. I fell, losing my footing, and jarred my elbow and hip. "Go, Benji! Help Ruby."

Benji whined when he saw I was down, but then careened towards Ruby.

Ruby rolled away just as the swan pecked at her. "Behave! Stop that! Bad swan. What has this creature got against me?"

The swan waddled after her, its wings out and head up. It truly seemed intent on destroying Ruby.

"Stop flapping your arms. You're scaring it." I'd got back on my feet, my hip throbbing from my hard landing. "Benji, herd the swan away from Ruby. Get the creature to the side of the road and guard it."

Benji barked at the swan, but the bird ignored him, determined to take down a snow-covered, soggy, squeaking Ruby.

I limped nearer to the swan. "Ruby, be quiet! The bird is injured. One of its wings is held at an unnatural angle, and it's limping almost as badly as me."

"I'm the injured one. It nipped me. More than once." Ruby wiped snow off her face. "Veronica, you're the animal whisperer. Do something! Talk this swan down from its quest for revenge."

The swan hissed and lunged at Ruby. She shuffled back, using her hands and feet to propel herself away from the swan's beak.

"You distract it, and I'll catch it." I tugged off my coat and instantly regretted it, but it was the only thing I had close at hand to capture the swan without getting pecked, and I needed something to restrain its wings.

"It needs no distraction. It's focused on me. Every time I move, it matches me." Ruby got to her feet, but they slipped from underneath her and she landed in the snow with a loud, unladylike grunt.

The swan took its opportunity and jumped on her. I jumped at the same time, covered the bird with my coat, wrapped it around its middle, then hooked one arm around its neck while clamping the beak shut with my free hand.

"Now, what's all this nonsense? Everyone likes Ruby, and she's done you no harm. She didn't mean to drive at you and scare you."

The swan was lighter than I'd expected, and it barely struggled as I adjusted my grip to make sure we were both comfortable and its wings and legs were tucked in.

Ruby clambered to her feet, aided by Benji, who had hold of her coat collar and was tugging it. She glared at the swan as she swiped ineffectively at her snow-covered coat. "Is suggesting roast swan for Christmas crass?"

"And illegal. This could be one of the King's birds. Although if it is, it looks rather sad and dishevelled." My brow furrowed as I studied the defeated bird. "We'll have to take it with us."

"To Mrs Bell's house? You can't! It'll fight back. Leave it in the car," Ruby said.

"It'll panic in there on its own," I said. "It comes with us. It's not struggling. I think it's appreciating my body warmth, which is rapidly vanishing. Did it really peck you?"

"It got in several nips. I'll survive. I've had much worse." Ruby abandoned her coat cleaning task and rubbed at the red welt on her hand. "Is the poor bird really hurt?"

"It must be why it's out in these conditions. And from the weight of it, the creature is most likely desperate for food. I doubt it can fly with its wing like this." I tucked the swan carefully against my unbruised hip. "Let's hope Mrs Bell is an animal lover, because she's getting a new house guest."

It took another twenty minutes and some soldier-like cursing from both of us before we reached Mrs Bell's small, sturdy stone cottage, the thatch adorned with a layer of snow. The thick walls of the cottage were painted white, a warm glow emanating from within, hinting at a most welcome fire. I couldn't have hoped for more.

Ruby rapped loudly on the wooden front door, and it was opened a few seconds later by a wide-eyed woman with a round face.

"Mrs Bell?" I asked and made the introductions.

"Have you ladies taken leave of your senses? I didn't expect your visit after the weather took a turn for the worse." Mrs Bell's gaze settled on the bundled swan. "Oh! What have you got there?"

"This is our version of the Christmas goose," Ruby said. "You're welcome to roast the beast."

"No swans get roasted in our version of the Christmas Carol," I said hurriedly. "We found this injured bird on the road. May we bring it inside? I fear it'll perish if we leave it in the snow."

Mrs Bell's mouth opened and closed several times, and she stared at us before snapping back to her senses. "Come in, both of you. The bird and the dog, too. You're soaked through, so you must be freezing. Take off your shoes and coats and leave them here. I don't want you dripping all over my floor. And wipe your dog's paws."

I nodded, easing off my damp shoes, and waited until Ruby was shoe and coat free before carefully handing her the swan. Then I wiped Benji down with an old towel provided by Mrs Bell and took off my sodden coat.

Mrs Bell studied the swan from a safe distance. "I don't know what I'll do with that."

"It needs somewhere warm and secure, something to drink, and food. Grains or vegetables are best." I took the swan off Ruby, since it had begun to hiss at her and struggle.

"I have leftover vegetable stew. It's plain. No herbs. Will that do?" Mrs Bell asked.

"That will be perfect."

She puffed out her ruddy cheeks, then nodded. "Follow me. I have an old dog cage in the back. I used to have a sheep dog. Wonderful animal. I miss him terribly. We can settle the bird in there, close to the fire, and give it some peace."

After Mrs Bell had set up the dog cage, I got Ruby to hold the bird's beak and neck while I inspected its injuries. It wasn't fighting. It was too tired, and allowed me to test its legs, feet, and wings.

"How badly is it injured?" Mrs Bell brought through clean towels and a tray with a pot of tea and some homemade mince pies.

"The wings aren't broken, but the bird may have collided with something. It has cuts on its chest. I doubt it can fly," I said. "He's in a very sorry state."

"It's a boy?" Ruby asked.

"I'm not a swan expert, but he has a wide wing span, and he's bigger than the one we have."

"You have a pet swan?" Mrs Bell asked.

"No, we found one injured while in London," I said. "We're taking care of her."

"This chap could be a regular from our pond." Mrs Bell stood with her hands on her hips, taking in the scene. "The swans are a feature of Little Kennington. We ring them, so we know they're local. Check its leg."

A quick inspection revealed a small ring around the bird's right leg. "This is one of yours."

"Those proud creatures wander around the village without a care in the world. Although the last time I saw them doing their daily parade, there were only six."

"Oh! Then we may have the missing one," Ruby said.

"If that's the case, she's a long way from home," I said.

"It's this weather," Mrs Bell said. "Someone brought one back from five miles away. The silly creature got turned around when the snow hit and went off in the wrong direction."

"There's a ring on our swan's leg," I said. "It's the same colour as this one."

"No wonder this fellow is so distressed. Other than a young one in the group, we have three pairs. They don't always get along, but I believe they're related, so they tolerate each other. And our pond is big, so they have their own areas." Mrs Bell pursed her lips. "Some of the villagers feed them, but with the weather getting bad, there haven't been as many going outside. Maybe that's why this one is so hungry."

"Or he could be looking for his missing mate," Ruby said.

"Swans eat mainly vegetation from the pond bed, but pickings will be slim with the extreme cold. If the pond is frozen over, he'd have struggled to get a decent meal." I settled the bird into the cage.

"He can make up for it now." Mrs Bell had already placed food down for him.

I dried my hair with a borrowed towel as the swan gobbled the food, watching with satisfaction. The fact the bird had a healthy appetite was a positive sign.

"Take a seat, ladies. I know I promised you a festive sherry, but I thought you'd need warming after your travels. I'll pour. You didn't walk here, did you? Aren't you staying somewhere in London with the Drapers? I know they had a problem with their heating, so had to relocate at the last minute." Mrs Bell gestured to chairs close to the fire before taking her own seat.

"We drove most of the way." Ruby settled into a comfy chair with a knitted blanket folded over the back. "We left the car when the road became too treacherous."

I lifted my eyebrows. "We almost hit the swan. Ruby's car is stuck in a ditch."

"Oh, my. You ladies have had an adventure." Mrs Bell handed around welcome cups of steaming tea and the delicious mince pies dusted with icing sugar. "Since you've made the journey in such awful conditions, you must be keen to learn about John."

"As I mentioned, he was found outside the tavern we're staying in. It was a shock."

"I imagine so." Mrs Bell drew in a breath. "It's sad what happened, but I must admit, I was having second thoughts about keeping him as my lodger."

"Why was that?" Ruby attempted to dry her shoes by holding them close to the open flames.

"He was charming and amusing, but terrible with his money. And he was behind on paying me my rent, and not just by a couple of weeks." Mrs Bell set down her cup.

"John had money trouble?" I asked.

"I fear so, although he didn't say as much to me. I'm not unsympathetic when someone is struggling. I take in lodgers because I'm on my own. My dear husband was lost in the Great War, and he left little in the way of savings. I was worried I'd have to find somewhere cheaper to live, but then I decided to rent the spare rooms. I've had several lodgers, and when John made his application, he seemed ideal. He had a job and a good reference, and he said all the right things when I interviewed him. Father Bumble even put in a good word for him."

"But it didn't go as planned, and he stopped paying rent?" I asked.

"At first, he was only a day or two late with his payment. John said his employer was unreliable, and he was looking for another job with a steadier income. But then, a few days turned into a week." Mrs Bell smoothed a hand over her practical brown skirt. "He owes me almost a month's back rent. I can't afford to keep him. And I provide his meals, too. I decided that after Christmas, if he was unable to pay me what he owed, I'd ask him to leave."

"I'm sorry to hear that," I said. "Your cottage is lovely, though. You'll have no trouble filling the room."

"I need to clear his belongings first, and that'll have to wait until after Christmas." Mrs Bell hesitated. "I was hoping there might be something I could sell to make back a little of what I'm owed. Do you think that would be allowed?"

"From what I've heard, John had no family, and he wasn't married, so there isn't anyone who'll want his personal effects," I said.

Mrs Bell gave a little snort. "No offence to the recently departed, but what young woman would have him after what happened with his last lady friend?"

Ruby set down her shoes and tackled a mince pie with vigour. "What did he do to her?"

"I don't like to gossip, but I overheard a few things after church," Mrs Bell said. "John had a young lady, and she waited for him while he was fighting in the war. When he came home, they continued their courtship, and she invited John to meet her parents."

"Did John do something to offend them?" I asked.

"It can't be proven, but two days after John visited the family in Kent, their house was broken into and some silver stolen."

"That could have been an unfortunate coincidence." Ruby glanced at me and raised her eyebrows.

"I'd be tempted to agree, but a week later, John came into money. He paid me everything he owed and a little bonus as a way of apologising. And he was seen drinking in the pub and playing cards." Mrs Bell sniffed. "I don't agree with gambling, but it was his favourite pastime. I warned him no good would come of it."

"What happened to the girl he was involved with?" I asked.

"She left him! They had a terrible argument, and she accused him of taking her parents' silver. They haven't spoken since."

"Does the girl live in the village?" Perhaps this mistreated girlfriend had returned to make John pay for stealing from her family.

"No, she moved back to be with her parents," Mrs Bell said. "The last I heard, she had no interest in staying here. She only visited because this was John's home. And it's a small village, so it's impossible to avoid bumping into people you don't want to."

"What job did John move on to?" I asked. "I'm aware he used to work at Morbid and Poe, but it didn't suit him."

Mrs Bell lifted her gaze to the ceiling. "That's another thing I found out from my church ladies. Again, I'm not gossiping, but I became concerned I'd never get the money owed to me, so I asked around to see if people knew where John was employed. I thought I'd speak to his new employer and see if we could come to an arrangement so he would pay me the rent directly from John's wages."

"Did John lie to you about having a new job?" Ruby swiftly accepted another mince pie from the plate Mrs Bell offered her.

"He had a job at the factory you mentioned when he first moved to the village, but he was let go after a few weeks. John never told me he'd lost that job, but it makes sense, since he couldn't afford to pay me his rent."

"Have you seen anyone causing John trouble?" I asked.

"He didn't have many visitors stop by here. I believe he conducted his business in the pub. But it's no use going there to ask questions. They're closed because of the bad weather. Their pipes froze, and I don't think they'll open for a few days." Mrs Bell shuffled forward in her seat. "Why are you so interested in John? Did he owe you money, too?"

"No, it's nothing like that. We met him for the first time at the Drapers Christmas gathering," I said.

"Mrs Draper has such a generous heart. She always donates to our collections. And these mince pies are from the hamper she gave me."

"Mitzie invited John to spend Christmas with them. Since he was new to the village, she didn't want him to be on his own."

"How very like her. She's always worrying about other people."

"Mitzie is a good person," I said.

"It's a shame the same can't be said for John. I tried to think the best of him, but the more I learned about the man, the more I realised I'd made an error in opening my home to him."

"You could be right." I glanced at Ruby, and she nodded at me to continue. So far, we'd not mentioned any foul play. "We're concerned John's death may not have been an accident."

Mrs Bell lifted a hand to her mouth, then sighed. "I warned that young man no good would come of his inappropriate friendships. Most of the men who drink at the pub are acceptable types, but John gravitated towards the troublemakers. Other gamblers who were usually passing through, looking for an easy way to make money. I tried to get him to join the church, but he paid me no attention. Now this has happened. That poor man."

"It is a tragedy," I said. "You can understand why we're curious."

"What about the police?"

"They've been asking questions, but their minds are on other things."

"If it's the lot who look after Little Kennington, they're not much good." Mrs Bell tutted and offered more tea.

We sipped our tea and ate more fruity mince pies, warmth seeping through damp clothing as we watched the swan hunt for more food. He seemed content in his cage, although he was most likely simply relieved to be out of the blizzard and to have food in his belly. I felt the exact same way.

"Would you mind if we inspected John's room?" I asked. "It may give us a clue as to why someone would want him dead."

Mrs Bell considered the question as she nibbled on a mince pie. "I suppose there would be no harm. But I don't want you taking anything. John has a debt to repay. I'm alone here, and he's my only lodger at the moment, so I need to get what I'm owed."

"We'll only peek at his belongings," Ruby said. "We promise we won't take anything."

Mrs Bell nodded. "Finish your tea, and then we'll take a look. Or would you like a sherry now?"

We drank our tea, accompanied by a small glass of sweet sherry, made sure the swan was settled, and then headed up the narrow wooden staircase that sat between the front parlour and kitchen at the back of the cottage.

"I sleep downstairs in the back room. My lodgers have the upstairs area," Mrs Bell said as she showed us the way. "This is John's room." She opened a door to reveal a compact room with a single bed, a small, scratched chest of drawers, and a chair. The bed was made and everything looked tidy.

"I'm assuming this is your work?" I gestured to the neatly made bed.

A smile brightened Mrs Bell's face. "Even though John served his country during the war and would have needed to keep everything neat, he rarely made his bed here. I don't mind, though. I like looking after my lodgers, even when they misbehave. It keeps me busy."

I stepped into the room with Ruby. There was a faint odour of lemon polish and everything was spick and span.

"There's little to see," Mrs Bell said. "John had a few clothes, which he stored in that chest, and there are photographs and notepads over there, but not much else. He said he liked to travel light."

I glanced at Ruby, then at Mrs Bell as she lingered by the door. "The swan seems to have taken to you."

Mrs Bell settled her hands under her bosom. "It may have done, but it's not staying. Don't get any ideas in your head about lumbering me with the creature."

"I wouldn't dream of such a thing. But perhaps you could get him more food? I'd hate to think of the bird going hungry. And you're practically neighbours, since he's also a Little Kennington resident! I can tell you look out for others."

"Well, I don't want the creature going without. I suppose your dog wants a biscuit as well?"

I smiled down at Benji, who had faithfully followed me up the stairs. "He never says no to a treat."

"I'll be back in a minute. Don't take anything." Mrs Bell huffed out a breath, then turned and her slippered footsteps pounded down the stairs.

"John was quick to make enemies while living here." Ruby rummaged through the chest.

"Stealing, gambling, lying to his lady. They're all good reasons for wanting him dead." I browsed the photographs on the nightstand and flicked through the notepads. The photographs were mainly of John in a soldier's uniform, standing with a group of other army recruits. They had the fresh-faced look of soldiers who had yet to see the true horror of war.

"What about Mrs Bell?" Ruby asked.

"As John's killer?" I stared hard at the photographs.

"He owed her money."

"Mrs Bell has a good heart. Many people wouldn't have let us inside with a wild animal, dripping wet, and talking about murder, but she barely batted an eyelid."

"I suppose it's not a large amount of money. I certainly wouldn't kill for it," Ruby said.

I lifted a photograph and studied it, my heart skipping a beat. Despite my damp clothing, I grew hot, then cold, then hot again. "Oh, my."

"What is it? Have you found something?"

I held out the photograph. "Ruby! I know who killed John."

# Chapter 17

"You can't risk going out in these conditions!" Mrs Bell fretted around us as we prepared to leave her cottage. "You'll never make it back to the Swan Tavern on foot."

Ruby gave me a worried look, but I shook my head. "Time isn't on our side."

Mrs Bell fussed some more. "I have spare rooms you can stay in. And the swan can stay, too. We'll figure out what to do with it in the morning."

"We must get back," I said. "Do you have a car we might borrow?"

Mrs Bell's hand fluttered against her chest. "My late husband sold his vehicle before he went to war. There's only his hobby tractor out the back."

"A hobby tractor?" Ruby cocked her head, the concern on her face fading. "Does it still run?"

"That old thing never breaks down. Neither should it, considering the amount of time and love he smothered it with. I always said that tractor was his mistress."

"Mrs Bell, could we borrow your tractor?" Ruby smiled at me, a gleam of excitement in her eyes.

"You can drive a tractor? Were you in the Land Army?"

"Not exactly. But I have experience using large machinery," Ruby said.

"It's the perfect vehicle to get us back to town safely," I said. "Tractors can get through anything."

"And we'll bring it back in one piece as soon as possible," Ruby said.

"Oh, I don't know. It's not proper for young ladies to ride around on a tractor when it's dark and snowing. And it hasn't been used in over a month, so it may not even start. I get a lad from the village to ensure the parts don't seize, but that doesn't mean it's roadworthy."

"You just admitted it's a solid metal work horse. Have no fear. Ruby once drove a tank," I said.

"A tank I stole!" Ruby chuckled at Mrs Bell's astonished expression.

"We must get back to the tavern," I said, "and let our friends know what's going on. And it's Christmas Eve. They'll worry if we don't return soon."

Mrs Bell's eyes narrowed. "Did you find something useful in John's belongings?"

"Rest assured, we took nothing. It's all yours," Ruby said. "John had some nice clothes, so you should get money for them. And I noticed a pocket watch, too. That'll be worth a few shillings to the right person."

"I suppose that's something. But do you have to leave?" Mrs Bell's concerned gaze went to the window, where a blanket of white swirled past, whipped around by a biting wind.

"It's imperative. Please, let us borrow your tractor," I said.

She sighed. "I have no use for it. But promise me you'll be careful."

"I've never crashed a tractor yet," Ruby said.

Mrs Bell gasped. "How many tractors have you driven?"

Ruby chuckled. "This will be my first. But it can't be any trickier than a stolen tank."

Mrs Bell hesitated in the doorway, then strode off and returned with a set of keys. "What about your swan?"

"He's settled and asleep," I said, after ducking my head into her warm kitchen to peek at the bird. "Would you be so kind as to keep him here overnight? When we come back with the tractor, we'll bring the other swan and reunite them. That way, we can see if they know each other."

Mrs Bell stared at the caged bird and sighed again. "If I must. But if it makes any mess, I'll expect it to be cleaned up by both of you. I don't care if it is Christmas Day. You'll be on your hands and knees with water and soap."

"Thank you. And Merry Christmas." I impulsively kissed her cheek and pressed a few coins into her hand for her trouble. "You're an angel."

She shooed us away. "Off you go. And don't get yourselves into any more trouble. I won't be able to sleep for worrying."

"Don't fret about us. We're made of stern stuff." Ruby followed Mrs Bell through the small kitchen to a back door. A flurry of snow blasted in as she opened it.

Mrs Bell backed away as we swiftly put on coats and shoes. "Are you sure you won't change your minds?"

"We're convinced this is our only course of action," I said. "Which way to your tractor?"

"Follow the path and turn right. It's inside the shed. You can't miss it."

After thanking Mrs Bell again, we dashed through the snow, Benji at my side.

"What a stroke of luck," Ruby said. "We'll be back in no time to catch our killer."

"I just hope our killer's conscience is big enough that he comes clean," I said. "We don't have much evidence."

"We've got enough. He won't get away with it." Ruby unlocked the shed and gasped. Sitting in front of us was a small, sturdy green tractor with a steel frame and large, spoked wheels.

"I hope it's got petrol." I studied the vehicle.

Ruby patted the sloping hood and then hopped up into the leather seat. "She's a little underwhelming. I was imagining something bigger."

"Mrs Bell said it was a hobby tractor. In you get, Benji. You can sit between us. And there's a petrol can over there should we need it." I pointed to the corner of the shed.

Once we were all seated, Ruby inhaled. "Wish me luck." She inserted the key and turned over the engine. It rumbled to life with the grumbling purr of a machine that had been beautifully cared for.

"We've just received an early Christmas gift," I said. "Good work Mr Bell for showering this machine with so much affection."

"Let's see how she moves." Ruby tested the gears, then eased the tractor out of the shed.

As we turned onto the snowy lane that would take us back to the Swan Tavern, I waved at Mrs Bell, who stood in the front doorway. She lifted her hand and then hurried back inside, closing the door to keep out the chill.

The tractor was small but powerful, and we were soon motoring past Ruby's stranded car, making excellent progress.

"How will you handle things when we get to the tavern?" Ruby asked.

"Swiftly. We'll gather everyone in the billiard room and reveal all. Then we'll stand back and let the killer ease his guilty conscience." I snuggled Benji close to my side.

"And if he doesn't step forward and do the right thing?"

"We'll keep digging. But once we reveal what we found in John's room, the killer will have to come clean."

The rest of the journey was spent huddled together, enduring the cold as our teeth chattered. The tractor was only mildly warmer than an icebox, and the retro-fitted cover and doors had gaps that allowed the chilled wind to blast through and freeze our still damp clothing.

But the snow was easing, and by the time we reached the busier London streets, visibility had improved, and Ruby only had three near misses as we traversed the roads back to the tavern.

"You can't drive that thing around here!" someone yelled as we passed.

I waved at them. "Why not? It's Christmas."

"I won't be able to park this beast behind the tavern," Ruby said. "We'll have to leave it on the street."

"It'll be safe enough out there. The shops are closing soon since it's Christmas Eve, and everyone wants to be inside with their loved ones, not stealing farm machinery," I said.

"Which is exactly where we should be," Ruby said. "Murder at Christmas is just not on."

"I couldn't agree more. That's why we'll resolve this mystery tonight, so we can enjoy ourselves tomorrow."

We did our best to park the tractor as inconspicuously as possible, no mean feat given its size and colour, then leapt out and dashed to the entrance of the Swan Tavern, the warm lights a welcome sight.

Baxter opened the door as we arrived. He looked at us, then at the tractor, and tilted his head. "Pleasant afternoon, ladies?"

"A most wonderful afternoon," Ruby said. "Baxter, would you be so kind as to gather everyone in the billiard room this instant?"

"The ladies as well?"

"Everyone in our party." I shrugged off my damp coat. "This is a special occasion."

Baxter took our coats and nodded. "I'll make the necessary arrangements. Perhaps you would like to change first. And are hot drinks required? Hot water bottles, too?"

"Thank you, but there's no time for that," I said. "How did Tiberius behave while we were gone?"

"He's a good boy. Absolutely no trouble. He's asleep in your room."

"I wouldn't mind changing my shoes," Ruby said to me. "My toes are numb to the bone."

"Very well. Baxter, give us two minutes, and we'll join everyone shortly." I dashed up the stairs with Ruby and Benji. I greeted Tiberius, smoothed my hair into the semblance of a style, and changed into clean stockings and shoes. Then it was back down the stairs and into the billiard room.

Baxter, being his usual efficient self, had ensured everyone was there. Eddie and Mitzie sat together. Father Bumble stood by the fireplace with his back to the welcome warmth. Devon inspected the books on the shelf. Baxter stood by the door, alert and ready to fulfil anyone's request.

"Excellent. You're all here," I said.

"What's going on, Vale?" Eddie asked. "Mitzie has arranged party games and refreshments for everyone this evening before we head to Midnight Mass. We don't want to make a hash of things and stop the fun. There's been enough of that already."

"We can enjoy all of that, and we'll have plenty of time for the church service, but we have the matter of John's murder to discuss," I said. "We've just returned from an eventful meeting with John's landlady, Mrs Bell."

"Still snooping, I see." Eddie's expression hardened.

"Naturally. You know, I can never resist a mystery."

"Shall I leave you to it?" Baxter asked.

"Please, stay. Everyone should hear this," I said. "We all knew John. But perhaps you could close the door, Baxter. We don't need any of the tavern's staff to overhear how this tragedy unfolded."

He nodded and did as instructed, remaining standing in front of the door.

I looked around the assembled party. Not all the original suspects were here, but the most pertinent ones were. "I have proof that someone in this room murdered John."

There were several gasps. Eddie made the most remarkable spluttering noises, but before he could form any objection, I pressed on, focusing on Devon. "You were seen arguing with John not long before he was found dead."

Devon blinked several times. "I've admitted that. We argued over a girl."

"Perhaps that was one concern you had about him, but your argument at the ice rink had nothing to do with a lady. And John wasn't seeing anyone. He had been involved with a young lady he'd taken up with before he went to war, but when he returned, there was a misunderstanding and she separated from him."

Devon's forehead crumpled. "That's ... yes, that's what the fight was about. John had several women on the go, and that's not the behaviour of a gentleman. I pulled him up on it and told him to stop gadding about."

A knock at the main door of the tavern made me tense. Baxter left the room, and a moment later, Inspector Harold Finchley and Sergeant Brown appeared.

"Good evening, everyone. Apologies for interrupting your Christmas Eve gathering, but we had reports of a tractor being driven recklessly through the snow and abandoned outside the tavern by two well-dressed ladies. Does anyone here have information about that?" Inspector Finchley's gaze was on me and Ruby.

"A tractor! Are you out of your mind?" Eddie exclaimed.

"It belongs to us," Ruby said. "Well, we were kindly loaned the tractor by a wonderful woman. And I wasn't driving recklessly. I was in full control for the majority of the time. And I hit nothing and no persons."

"Why would anyone loan you a tractor?" Mitzie was breathless with surprise.

"Mrs Bell lent us the tractor after my car spun off the road when we almost hit a swan," Ruby said. "An attacking swan! Although I forgave him when I realised he was injured and heartbroken."

Everyone stared at Ruby, most of their expressions full of disbelief.

"You can't drive recklessly through the streets of London on Christmas Eve, ploughing into snowbanks for jollies. Do you even know how to operate a tractor safely?" Inspector Finchley's face was pink with indignation.

Ruby stood tall and placed her hands on her hips. "Of course I know how to drive one! I just brought us safely back from Little Kennington in said vehicle. There's the evidence, not that I should need to present any to you. I'm an excellent driver."

"And if Christmas Eve is an inappropriate day for our misbehaviour, please advise us as to what days are more appropriate for reckless tractor fun?" I asked.

Inspector Finchley's cheeks flushed. "None! We had several complaints. It's not proper."

"I'm intrigued, Inspector. The matter of mildly reckless tractor driving caused you to arrive so speedily, yet when one of our party was murdered, you barely put in an appearance," I said. "One wonders about the local constabulary's priorities, since Inspector Templeton was dismissed."

Inspector Finchley tugged at his collar. "It's not like that. You were informed of the train crash. And as I'm sure Colonel Draper has told you by now, John Robinson's death has been recorded as accidental. That required less haste."

"And I'm certain when his autopsy is completed, your experts will discern that the marks on his wrists and face weren't caused by a fall. As I was just telling the assembled party, we know who killed John," I said.

Inspector Finchley looked stunned. "Has someone confided in you?"

"No confiding was required. We looked for the clues and found them. The killer is in this room."

Devon shook his head, his expression tense. "And as I was explaining to Veronica, it wasn't me!"

"You haven't been honest with us, though, have you?" I asked. "Your fight with John at the park had nothing to do with a woman."

Devon's anxious gaze flicked around the party. "Does it matter what the argument was about?"

I arched an eyebrow and waited him out.

Devon rolled his shoulders. "I'll admit, our dispute wasn't about a lady. It was my own stupid fault for thinking I was helping a chap when he was down on his luck. It turns out I'm not as smart as many consider me to be."

"What did you do?" I asked.

"I ... I made the mistake of loaning John money," Devon finally said after several seconds of fumbling with his shirt cuffs. "He'd lost his job and had a string of bad hands when playing cards, so I took pity on him. The man had a silver tongue when he wasn't drunk, and John said he had another job lined up and he'd pay me back as soon as he could."

"Let me guess. He never did?"

"Correct. John even had the cheek to ask for more. He also tried to place a wager with me to win back some of the money, but he had nothing to put down! I made an error once, and I wasn't doing it again. I was embarrassed to admit I'd been duped by him, so I told you we argued about a woman."

"Did you have a hand in his demise, sir?" Inspector Finchley asked.

"No! I wanted nothing more to do with the man. He'd been a nuisance ever since moving to Little Kennington."

I turned to Eddie and Mitzie. "You've made your feelings about John clear, Colonel."

His nostrils flared. "What of it?"

"And you have a temper as fiery as a blazing furnace."

"It's got me into a scrape or two, but being with Mitzie has settled me." He patted the hand she had resting on his arm. "And what does my temper have to do with John's death?"

"Veronica, you can't possibly point the finger at my husband," Mitzie said. "We were together that day. Not that I think for one second you would kill someone, darling."

"Absolutely not! Well, only when serving my country," Eddie firmly stated.

"Eddie was jealous of John's interest in you," I said to Mitzie. "And having worked together, I know Eddie misses nothing when it comes to you. He adores you, and he'll do anything to keep you safe and happy."

"Not murder a chap!" Eddie smoothed down his moustache. "Well, perhaps if he did something unforgiveable, I might. But I didn't in this case. I had a poor opinion of the fellow, so I stayed away from him to avoid any clashes."

"Do you think Colonel Draper is the killer?" Inspector Finchley asked, somewhat hesitantly.

"No. Eddie didn't kill John, and neither did Mitzie. We've confirmed they were together when John was killed, purchasing tobacco at a shop close to the ice rink," I said.

"The cheek of it. You checked my alibi!" Eddie's cheeks grew red with indignation.

"You'd expect nothing less of me."

He grumbled some more before grudgingly nodding. "Well, get on with it. Who did it?"

I looked at Father Bumble, who had turned to the fire, his back to me. "Was John's confession in church so terrible you had to act upon his words?"

Mitzie gasped. "Now you think our priest did it! Veronica! Whatever has got into you?"

Father Bumble stopped rubbing his hands together, but remained looking at the fire.

"As the local priest, you said you hear extraordinary things from your parishioners," I said. "And they're always forgiven, as you advise people on how to move forward piously."

Father Bumble nodded. "I absolve people of their sins, as it should be. They learn their lesson and receive forgiveness."

"Not for John, though. The only way you could teach him a lesson was by ending his life," I said.

Father Bumble finally turned and looked at me, tears in his eyes. "You are mistaken. I ... I didn't kill him."

"But you didn't tell the truth about knowing him," I said. "We visited his lodgings, and Mrs Bell let us into his room. John had photographs of his time in service, and we were surprised to see you in one of them."

Father Bumble's jaw wobbled, and his gaze went to the door. "Perhaps ... yes, perhaps we did meet during the war. I ministered to so many men who served that I'm unable to remember every face."

"You were standing next to John in the photograph, and you had an arm around his shoulders," Ruby said. "You were more than passing acquaintances. Did you encourage him to move to Little Kennington after he left active duty? You hoped he would turn over a new leaf?"

Father Bumble glanced over my shoulder, his gaze still on the door as if he was considering an escape. Fortunately, the exit was blocked by both the police officers and Baxter. "A lot has happened since the war ended."

"You told us you didn't know him," Ruby said. "Why lie if you have nothing to hide?"

"Out with it, man," Eddie said. "What was your connection to John?"

"You knew him well enough to recommend him to Mrs Bell as a lodger," I said.

Father Bumble looked around the room, his expression growing frantic. "I knew there was goodness in him. John could change and repent his sins. At least, I hoped he would. But then I heard people talking about their homes being broken into and items taken."

"You thought it was John?" I asked.

"I didn't want to think the worst of him, but when we served together, there were rumours he was involved in a number of barracks thefts. More than a few of the men complained to me."

"Did you confront him?"

"I spoke to him about goodness and doing the right thing. The thefts stopped."

"But the habit was too hard to break," I said. "Once John was established in Little Kennington, he took up his old ways on your doorstep after you'd welcomed him here."

Father Bumble's shoulders slumped. "Even though John wasn't a regular churchgoer, he carried guilt. He came to confession and revealed he couldn't let go of a bad habit. I'm unable to tell you everything he revealed, though. That is between me, the confessor, and God."

"Is there anything you can share with us?" I asked.

Father Bumble drew in a shaky breath. "John promised to repent. He lied."

"How do you know that?" Inspector Finchley asked.

"The collection box meant for the orphanage this Christmas was stolen from the church. I saw John take it." Father Bumble bowed his head. "We've been collecting donations since November, and that money would have meant so much to the children."

I shook my head. "When John lost his job, he became desperate for money. He was sinking into debt and trouble was racing towards him, so he acted."

"He only lost his job because he stole from his employer, too." There was a touch of bitterness in Father Bumble's voice. "John couldn't see what he was doing was wrong. He thought he was owed a living, so he took what he felt he was entitled to. Nothing I said made him change his ways."

"So, you killed him?" Inspector Finchley took a step towards Father Bumble. "Are you confessing to John Robinson's murder?"

Father Bumble softly cleared his throat. "No. It wasn't me."

I twisted on my heel and faced Baxter, who'd remained silent throughout the conversation. "You told us the truth about your alibi, didn't you, Father? You were with Baxter on the day of the murder."

"Yes, we were together," Father Bumble whispered.

Baxter flinched, but said nothing.

"Doesn't that give both of them an alibi?" Mitzie asked.

"It would if they were both innocent," I said. "But not if they're both guilty."

# Chapter 18

"Veronica! Did you hit your head when Ruby crashed the car?" Mitzie clasped her husband's shoulder. "Baxter has been with us for years. You know him! And I trust him implicitly. I would know if he was a bad sort. Anyone who can keep my household running smoothly is sent by the angels."

"He is a solid chap," Eddie said. "We couldn't want for a better butler."

"And I don't disagree with his experience," I said. "Baxter is a flawless professional. But he's also a killer."

"Why do you think that?" Inspector Finchley was poised, desperate to make an arrest, but not knowing which suspect, if any, to tackle first.

I kept my attention on Baxter, who hadn't moved. Hadn't even taken a breath since I'd pointed the finger of blame at him. "Baxter, Father Bumble, and John were all in the photograph we found in John's lodgings."

"Did you serve together?" Eddie asked Baxter.

Baxter remained motionless and silent.

"I'm your employer, man, and I demand an answer! Did you know John from the war?"

He still didn't respond.

"Baxter, you must have been shocked when you discovered John had moved to Little Kennington, assisted by Father Bumble," I said. "I expect you hoped to never see him again."

"It … it was an accident," Father Bumble blurted out.

"John's death? How do you know? I demand an answer." A red flush crept up Eddie's neck as he failed to keep his anger in check. "Were you there when John died? Did Baxter do it?"

The priest's expression was sorrowful as he stared hard at Baxter, who kept his gaze fixed on the wall opposite him.

"Father Bumble was there to ensure no one saw what was going on while Baxter administered what he considered justice," I said. "After we'd discovered John's body and were all together in the tavern, Father Bumble comforted us. He was rubbing at a cocoa stain on his clothes, but he told us he'd returned here while we were skating to change. He didn't do that. He was acting as a lookout while Baxter ended John's life."

"Ended his life?" Inspector Finchley didn't appear to know what to do. If he was Jacob's replacement, I could well imagine the police station's criminal conviction rate plummeting.

Eddie stepped forward. "Father, would you place your hand on a Bible and declare Veronica is telling the truth? Baxter is the criminal?"

I was a trifle irked such a thing was needed, but Eddie held a bias towards Baxter's innocence.

Father Bumble opened and closed his mouth several times, then ducked his head. "John was a terrible man.

Wherever he went, crime followed him. Nothing would stop him from taking what didn't belong to him."

"Including when you served together," I said. "John was stealing from other soldiers, wasn't he? Or was it worse than that and he was taking supplies? Perhaps selling them on the black market?"

Father Bumble pressed his lips together as if forcing himself to remain silent.

"What did you see Baxter do to John?" Inspector Finchley asked Father Bumble.

"Nothing! I saw no one killed. I can state that with an honest heart."

Ruby shook her head. "Only because you had your back turned when the crime was committed. You had to ensure no one saw what was going on in the alley beside the tavern. But you were there, and you could have stopped Baxter from committing murder."

Father Bumble turned his face towards the fire. "Brave men died in the war because of John's disgraceful behaviour. His actions served only himself, and he cared nothing about where his stolen goods ended up."

"He was stealing more than a few pennies or gifts," I said. "It was Army supplies, too."

Father Bumble tried to catch Baxter's eye, both men staying silent, but Baxter's forehead was dotted with perspiration.

"A photograph of the men together during service is proof of little," Inspector Finchley said. "Especially not murder."

"That's true. And if it weren't for the injured swan we found under John's body, it's likely Baxter and Father Bumble would have got away with this," I said.

"A ... swan?"

"Exactly. Large white bird. Orange beak. Powerful."

"I know what a swan is!"

"Jolly good. That swan makes this puzzle fit together," I said. "When Baxter was serving hot cocoa and cake by the ice rink, I noticed injuries on his face and hand. When Mitzie asked about them, Baxter said he'd fallen in the snow, so I thought nothing of it. Most of us have had a slip while we've been here."

"I have," Mitzie said. "I have bruises in places where there shouldn't be bruises. Go on, Veronica. What do the marks prove?"

"Baxter's marks look like the red marks on Ruby's hand. They're the signs of a swan attack."

The only thing making a noise was the crackling fire. Everyone stared at me. Benji gave a small whine, followed by Tiberius.

"Did I hear you correctly?" Eddie regarded me with frank incredulity. "A swan revealed to you that Baxter is a killer?"

"It's true," Ruby said. "When I almost ran over the swan, it attacked me. The wretched creature got in a few good pecks before Veronica and Benji came to my rescue. A swan's beak is a vicious weapon. Take a look." She pulled up her sleeve to reveal three long, thin red scrapes with blueish tinges and a raised welt on her hand. "Now look at Baxter's hands and arms. We have matching injuries."

Baxter finally moved and placed his arms behind his back, linking his fingers together.

I nodded. "Baxter's injuries were caused when he attacked John and startled the swan, who was hiding in the tavern's alley."

"Why does this tavern keep a swan?" Inspector Finchley asked.

"We don't keep any fowl on the premises. This particular swan lives on the pond in nearby Little Kennington. It must have got knocked off course by the bad weather and was searching for food when the fight between Baxter and John occurred. In the confusion, the creature must have panicked and attacked Baxter. Then John fell and landed on the bird, and her wing was injured."

"And then we almost killed her heartbroken mate on our way to visit Mrs Bell and discover the connection between John, Father Bumble, and Baxter," Ruby said. "What a stroke of luck I was attacked!"

Baxter lifted a hand and touched a raised red mark on his forehead. He swallowed several times. "I thought I'd seen a ghost or an avenging angel when this huge white creature flew at me. I didn't have a chance to react before it pecked my face. It all happened so fast. And with the adrenaline pumping..."

"Is that a confession to John's murder?" Inspector Finchley asked.

Baxter's usually perfect posture sagged, and he leaned against the door. "John was rotten to the core. He started small, taking personal effects from other soldiers, but as his confidence grew, his targets became bigger. I caught him once, trying to sell a stolen radio. I confronted him, but he denied it had been taken from the barracks. He said he'd picked it up at a market and was trying to turn a profit."

"But you didn't believe him?" I asked.

"Not for a second. And after that, I watched him. John stole helmets and medical supplies. It meant men had to fight without proper equipment. There were unnecessary deaths because of him. John is the killer, not me, nor Father Bumble."

"Why didn't you report him to the military police?" Inspector Finchley asked.

"We were in the middle of a war! And it was chaos towards the end. Equipment and supplies were going missing or being stolen by the enemy, orders mislaid, and everyone was suffering from stress and exhaustion. Our commanding officer wasn't interested in tackling a petty thief when the enemy pounded on our door, threatening our nation's sovereignty. And I thought, after the war, I'd never have to deal with John again. I could forget him and move on."

"This is all my fault." Father Bumble almost whispered the words. "I found John in a shelter for homeless men. He was down on his luck and repentant about his crimes. He said his life was about to turn a corner because he'd found a job, but he needed somewhere safe to live. The shelter was full of men who were suffering and using alcohol excessively. I told John about Mrs Bell's rooms as an act of kindness."

"In the hope he wouldn't return to his old ways," I said.

"John had so much to look forward to," Father Bumble said. "He'd reunited with his young lady, he had employment, and I even negotiated a reduced rate of rent from Mrs Bell until John got established and had some savings. Then he spoiled things by stealing."

"When I knew he was living in Little Kennington and up to no good again, I couldn't let him get away with it. John had blood on his hands. The blood of decent men," Baxter said. "And he was unrepentant. The last straw was when he stole from the church. I had to act."

My exhale came out a touch shaky. "So, you made sure John paid for what he did."

Baxter lifted his chin. "And I'm not sorry I did."

"Oh, Baxter. How could you?" Mitzie said. "Where am I supposed to find a butler as incredible as you?"

I looked at Inspector Finchley. "If I were you, I'd make an arrest or two."

---

Jacob didn't sound startled as I'd told him about our adventures in snowy London. The telephone line had finally crackled back to life, and I was thrilled to be speaking to him on Christmas morning.

"I wondered what hijinks you'd get up to while I was away." His warm voice made me relax.

"We were trying for a quiet season, but life had other plans for us," I said.

"It often does. I'm glad you figured things out and caught the killer."

"It was all thanks to the swan."

"And your clever brain."

"It was a joint effort." I drew in a breath. I wanted to know Jacob's progress in his own investigation, but I was oddly reluctant to ask. What if it was bad news?

"Did Ruby wake you at dawn by bouncing on your bed?" Jacob asked. "I imagine she's like an overexcited child on Christmas morning."

"She usually is. Most years, Ruby stays with me and my mother, so I know how wretchedly early she gets up to look at the gifts. But she's not feeling too bright and is still in bed," I said. "I took her some tea. I hope she's not coming down with something. We have been out in freezing conditions more than we should, so she could have caught a chill."

"Ruby won't let a cold slow her." Jacob paused. "I have news."

My stomach tightened. "Good news? No, that was foolish. You're looking into whether my father jumped off a cliff, or he was pushed. Neither outcome is good."

The line crackled, and for a second, I lost Jacob.

"And ... the man said ... saw a photo ..."

My breath hitched. "Jacob. Please, repeat that. What man? What photograph? A photograph of my father?"

"Yes. Veronica, did you hear all of that?"

"No! What have you learned? Who has images of my father? They can't be recent. What did the photographs reveal?"

"Not ... said ... dead." The line faded to nothing.

I shook the line, twiddled the numbers, and tried all manner of pointless curses to spring the connection back into existence. It refused to cooperate.

A flush of irritation flickered through me. My foolish stalling meant I still didn't know what happened to my father. Why was I so scared to learn the truth? Because if my father had been murdered, I wouldn't stop until I'd administered justice. And when I did, I'd end up in the same situation as Baxter and Father Bumble, and I'd no doubt drag Ruby down with me. She was my stalwart best friend and had adored my father. If someone hurt him, she'd not stop until they were well and truly sorry.

"Goodness! I was coming to wish you a Merry Christmas, but your expression makes you look like a wild tigress about to strike." Mitzie stood in the doorway leading to the dining room, wearing a lovely pink dress, diamonds glittering in her earlobes. "Did the conversation with Jacob not go well?"

"Part of it was fine, but I lost him before we could finish." I had to take several deep breaths to calm myself. What had Jacob been trying to tell me?

"Oh bother! You can try again later. But for now, we must celebrate. And with Baxter gone, I'm terrified the meal will be a disaster."

I focused on the here and now, and not on the unknowable. Until I could speak to Jacob again, that was all I had control of. "The tavern staff are capable, and I'm paying them triple their usual day rate to help, so our meal will be divine. You have nothing to worry about."

"Still, I want to check everything, so I need your help. And Ruby's! Where is she?"

"I'll rouse her. Give us ten minutes, and we'll be at your disposal."

Mitzie skipped over and embraced me. "And let's have no more mystery talk. Today will be all about merriment and mirth. Merry Christmas, my dear friend."

"And to you." I returned her embrace, then headed off to see how Ruby was faring. I'd do my best not to dwell on the mystery, but it always had a habit of finding me.

# Chapter 19

Crystal glasses clinked, and the air in the dining room was merry with laughter and chatter as we assembled for a fine luncheon in the Swan Tavern to celebrate Christmas.

Benji and Tiberius had been allowed to join us, and were faithfully seated on either side of me, ever hopeful for a delicious morsel from the extravagant feast on the table. There were roast potatoes and boiled, a giant turkey, a side of beef, and goose, and heaps of steaming vegetables.

"If I may have everyone's attention." Eddie pushed back his chair, lightly tapping his crystal champagne glass. "We have our former butler, Baxter, to thank for this meal. He made the preparations and ensured we would have our favourite food to celebrate this day."

Mitzie sighed. "I know Baxter is a killer, but I will miss him terribly. He was an organisational whizz. He could turn his hand to anything."

"I'm sure if you put in a good word with the police, they'll take that into account when it comes to sentencing," I said. "Maybe give him a place in the prison kitchen."

Mitzie smiled at my acerbic tone. "Don't think I won't. Darling, do you have any connections in the prison system?"

"I fear not, my love. We'll find you another butler just as capable," Eddie said. "The police telephoned this morning. Baxter has confessed, and Father Bumble admitted to being his accomplice and luring John back to the tavern. They'll be spending Christmas in the cells."

"It'll be a lot longer than Christmas once the sentencing is complete," I murmured.

"It's where they belong," Devon said. "And I'm glad of it. For a moment, I thought Veronica was planning on having me taken away for the crime. It was a terrifying experience to find oneself under her fierce scrutiny!"

Ruby chuckled. "Veronica often has that effect on men."

I lifted one shoulder as I gently kicked her under the table. "You were our prime suspect for a short amount of time. I'm glad it wasn't you, since you do such commendable work."

"In future, I'll be sure to have my arguments in private, or at least where you can't see them." Devon raised a glass to me.

"I won't toast Baxter because that would be inappropriate," Eddie said. "He saw an injustice done and sought to remedy it. That was a terrible mistake, and one he'll spend the rest of his life regretting."

"I'm not sure he has any regrets," Ruby whispered to me. "Baxter saw John's true light and wanted it snuffed out."

I nodded my reply. Criminals were rarely rotten to the core, but acted on a different set of values than most people. John had believed he deserved the things he took. It was his way of surviving. And to Baxter, murder was the only option to ensure John could never harm anyone ever again.

Eddie lifted his glass higher. "Let's remember what today is all about. Merry Christmas to all of us and here's to a peaceful new year."

We responded with our own chorus of *Merry Christmas* as we touched glasses and shared smiles.

Ruby leaned over to me. She wore a stunning cream beaded dress, her bare arms covered in a pretty silk shawl. "I hate to rush us through our feast, but don't forget, we have an appointment to keep."

I chewed hurriedly and swallowed. "Goodness. Perhaps a Christmas miracle as occurred."

"Whatever do you mean?"

"Ruby Smythe reminding me about not being late."

She tutted at me and swatted my hand. "I've been working on improving my timekeeping."

"Keep it up. And I haven't forgotten. I mentioned to Mitzie that we'll need to disappear for an hour. She understands."

"I knew she would, since Mitzi believes in true love even more than I do. And we can't keep our star-struck lovers apart for much longer." There was a smile on Ruby's face.

"Will anything stop you believing?" Ruby's heart had been bounced around, trodden on, and broken several times, yet she kept looking for true love.

She considered my question. "I've decided to never stop the search. And I won't stop looking until I have it. But perhaps, it'll arrive in a surprise package. One I never imagined having. Isn't that exciting?"

"Exciting and brave." I admired my best friend's courage to follow her dream with such ardent determination.

Although I wanted to linger over the delectable food, we made our excuses after the main course, changed into warmer clothing, and headed outside, Benji and Tiberius with us.

The snow had stopped, and the air was crisp and still. A white blanket glistened under the bright early afternoon light.

Although it was beautiful, we didn't dither, still feeling the nip in the air, and hurried around the back of the tavern to collect our feathered companion for the journey back to Mrs Bell's cottage.

The healed swan waited for us inside the tavern's shed, stamping her webbed feet impatiently as if she knew she was about to be reunited with her mate.

"Merry Christmas!" Ruby said to the swan. "Please don't peck me."

The swan hissed but allowed us into the shed. I moved quickly, tossing a blanket over the bird to cover her eyes, and making sure her wings were neatly folded so there was no chance she could use them or her beak on us.

Ruby pulled in a wooden crate, and we carefully placed the swan inside, making sure she was comfortable. Then, between us, we carried the crate to the tractor we'd convinced Inspector Finchley to let us keep outside the tavern overnight.

It was no small task to lift the crate onto the tractor, but we were capable ladies, and the bird was soon settled between us.

With Benji on my lap and Tiberius squashed next to my feet, Ruby started the engine, and we were soon whizzing along the snowy streets towards Little Kennington.

"I do so enjoy Christmas." Ruby's cheeks were bright pink because of the biting cold, making her look even more radiant than usual. "It brings out the best in people."

"It didn't Baxter," I said. "Nor Father Bumble. He missed Midnight Mass because he was an accomplice to a murder at Christmas."

"Those two gentlemen are the exception. Just think, if we hadn't encountered that mean old swan, you'd never have figured out Baxter was the killer. I'm almost glad I got viciously pecked, since I had the clues on my body!"

"It was a stroke of luck." I placed a hand on the crate as Ruby tested the limits of the tractor's engine. I was glad the mystery was resolved. It was a shame Mitzie had lost her most beloved butler, but it was better for him to be behind bars than free to roam, administering his own form of unhinged justice.

The rest of the journey was full of chatter and the occasional off-key carol as we kept our spirits up. Fifteen minutes later, Ruby rumbled the tractor around the side of Mrs Bell's cottage and back into the shed with expert precision. By the time we'd climbed down and hoisted the swan onto the ground, Mrs Bell stood by the shed door.

She wore a smart, warm day dress with a fleck of red thread, a smile on her face. "Merry Christmas, ladies. You made it back to the tavern in one piece, I see. And you've brought me another guest!"

We returned her festive greeting as she welcomed the dogs with pats and peered in at the swan.

"My feathered guest is looking forward to being reunited with his mate." Mrs Bell nodded at the house. "It's almost as if he knew she was coming. He's been honking and stamping his feet for the last hour. Nothing I could do would settle him."

"How is the swan's wing?" I asked as we carried the crate closer to the cottage.

"I'm no expert in fixing broken swans, but it's looking good. There's been preening and stretching. And hissing! He has a temper on him, that one."

"I couldn't feel any broken bones when I examined him, so it was most likely a muscle strain. And his fierce mood will fade when he's united with his mate," I said.

"I was worried about him, so I spoke to our resident swan enthusiasts this morning at church." Mrs Bell stopped by the back door. "They came by after the service and examined him. They believe he can be released back to the pond. You'd be welcome to join us while we set him free."

"Oh, lets!" Ruby said. "We can release the birds at the same time and watch their joy as they come together."

"I thought you didn't like swans after you were attacked by one," I said.

Ruby pressed a gloved hand against her heart. "I'm a fan of everlasting love. And I'm excited to see these two back together."

Mrs Bell chuckled. "The villagers have already taken the other bird to the pond. Can you carry the crate over there between you? It's not far. If not, I can get one of the local lads to help."

"We're happy to oblige," I said.

We put our backs into it and staggered through the snow with the crate between us and the dogs running around us in circles, excited by the action. It was only a few minutes' walk before we saw a small group of people assembled around a large, frozen pond.

Mrs Bell made some quick introductions, and then it was all hands on deck.

"We've put a new roost over there, tucked out of the way, and there's plenty of food." A local resident introduced as Peg pointed out the locations around the pond. "The other swans are close by, but we'll watch over things for a few days. Wild birds can be vicious if they spot weakness, although they won't have forgotten these two in such a short amount of time. From what Mrs Bell has told me, they've been on an adventure."

"They have. And I'm certain they'll appreciate your help to ensure their lives remain settled," I said.

"Let's waste no more time. Everyone, we're about to release the swans! On my mark." Peg nodded at me. "Ready. Go."

Both birds were set free, the doors on the cage and crate opened. It took a few seconds, but the swans waddled out of their respective confinements and onto the compacted snow. The moment they saw each other, the larger swan made a repetitive snort, while the female copied him. They snorted at each other several times, then touched beaks before rubbing necks.

Ruby breathed out a sigh. "That's true love in action."

The swans turned and regarded the group. We had wisely moved back to a safe distance, and I had hold of Benji and Tiberius. Then the birds tilted their heads before striding in that familiar waddle-wiggle of any large bird to the edge of the pond. After discovering the food left for them, they set about it with vigour, completely ignoring us.

"I call that a success," Mrs Bell said.

Peg nodded. "They're reunited again, so they'll have a happy Christmas. And we'll continue to be their guardians for as long as they need us."

"Shall we go back to my house? I have tea and iced fruit cake for everyone," Mrs Bell said.

We all agreed that was an excellent idea.

Peg fell into step with me as we headed to Mrs Bell's cottage. "Thank you for helping with the birds. There aren't many people around here who have time to protect the local wildlife."

"You're welcome. I'm experienced with looking after injured animals. I assist with stray dogs and cats when I find them in difficult circumstances." I gestured to Tiberius.

"You should visit Veronica's home this Christmas," Ruby said. "It's a veritable menagerie of odd creatures. She even had three parrot lodgers once. One of them was almost as vicious as that swan back there. He was a huge macaw rescued when his owner was arrested for armed robbery."

Peg's eyes widened. "Is that so? Are you a collector of the exotic?"

"No, I'm simply soft-hearted when it comes to animals. And I never turn away a sad, furry face that has nowhere to go," I said. "I help at the dogs' home in Battersea whenever I have the opportunity."

Peg clasped her hands together, a hopeful smile on her face. "I was hoping you'd be an animal lover. Mrs Bell told me about your visit on Christmas Eve and what you did for our injured swan, so I was intrigued to meet you."

"Do you like animals, too?" I asked.

"Absolutely." Peg glanced around. "And I'm in desperate need of your help. You see, I've got a situation with a deceased friend and a pining German Sheppard."

I shook my head. After Christmas, I needed time with Jacob to resolve the issue surrounding my father's death.

Ruby nudged me. "Veronica! You can't turn your back on an unwanted animal. It's Christmas!"

"I'm well aware of the time of year and the holiday we celebrate," I said, "but work will keep me busy."

Peg's expression dimmed. "They want to put him to sleep. He's a healthy dog, just a handful. I'd have him, but he's already knocked me over twice, and I've got two children to think about."

I hesitated. "Where is the dog currently living?"

"He's staying on a farm, but it doesn't suit him. And they can only keep him for a few weeks."

Ruby nudged me again.

I let out a gentle sigh. "After Christmas, I'll see if we have room at the dogs' home."

Peggy stopped and hugged me. "You're an angel to the animals."

"I do my bit."

After we'd exchanged contact details, Peg hurried off to let her friends know the German Sheppard had a future.

Ruby linked her hand around my elbow. "Everyone gets the happy ending they deserve."

"And the punishment, too."

"While we're solving cases that flummox the police, that'll always happen." She bit her bottom lip. "And now you have Jacob to assist for when I'm not around."

"Where are you going? Are you planning another holiday?"

"No! But work and my family keep me busy. I don't want to let you down."

I glanced at her. "You never do. And just because I have a friendly connection with Jacob—"

"A romantic connection. There's a difference."

"Very well. Romantic."

Ruby squeaked.

"Sensibly romantic. There'll always be a place for you. You're my dearest friend. That will never change."

Ruby drew in a breath, then shook her head. "You're right. I'm being silly."

"You're never that." I slowed and studied her expression. "Are you sure there's nothing troubling you?"

She squeezed my arm. "Not a thing. How about you?"

There was so much I wanted to share about what Jacob was getting up to, but until I had cold hard facts, there was no point in getting anyone's hope up.

"The same. Now, where is that fruitcake?"

# Historical notes

**Swan Tavern:** Death at the Swan Tavern has taken geographical liberties to ensure the book's tavern, which is based on a real pub in London, was within easy reach of the public outdoor skating rink the festive party visits.

The fictional Swan Tavern is loosely based on a London establishment that opened in 1861. The modern-day pub is still full of charm and character and is a popular place for tourists, although there are no murky alleys where dark deeds occur and cads meet a tragic end!

To see pictures of the tavern today, go here – https://www.swanec3.co.uk/gallery

**Ice skating in the 1920s:** Ice skating has been popular since the 1100s, with people using lakes and rivers when they froze over. In the nineteenth century, experiments began to make ice and indoor rinks were invented in London.

In 1876, John Gamgee opened the first mechanically frozen ice rink on the King's Road in Chelsea. It had a floor of pipes that circulated freezing liquid that cooled a mixture of water and glycerine above.

Fortunately, Veronica Vale's adventures occur after the creation of the artificial ice rink in Marylebone, where pig lard was used to make the surface slippery. Imagine the stench!

**Little Kennington**

This charming village arrived entirely from my imagination but is based on the visits I've taken over the years to delightful English villages. I put all of my favourite things in one place: a duck pond, thatched cottages, kindly, nosy neighbours, pretty shops, and lovely green spaces.

# Also by

Death at the Fireside Inn
Death at the Drunken Duck
Death at the Craven Arms
Death at the Dripping Tap
Death at the Harbour Arms
Death at the Swan Tavern
Death at the Jolly Cricketer

More mysteries coming soon. While you wait, why not investigate K.E. O'Connor's back catalogue (Kitty's alter ego.)

# About the author

Immerse yourself into Kitty Kildare's cleverly woven historical British mysteries. Follow the mystery in the Veronica Vale Investigates series and enjoy the dazzle and delights of 1920s England.

Kitty is a not-so-secret pen name of established cozy mystery author K.E.O'Connor, who decided she wanted to time travel rather than cast spells! Enjoy the twists and turns.

Join in the fun and get Kitty's newsletter (and secret wartime files about our sleuthing ladies!)

**Newsletter:** https://BookHip.com/JJPKDLB
**Website:** www.kittykildare.com
**Facebook:** www.facebook.com/kittykildare